VILLA
BUNKER

Originally published in French as *Villa Bunker* by Éditions P.O.L, Paris, 2009

Copyright © 2009 by Éditions P.O.L
Translation © 2013 by Andrew Wilson

First edition, 2013

Library of Congress Cataloging-in-Publication Data

Brebel, Sébastien.
[Villa bunker. English]
Villa bunker / Sebastien Brebel ; Translated by Andrew Wilson. -- First Edition.
pages cm
Originally published in French as Villa Bunker by Editions P.O.L, Paris, 2009.
ISBN 978-1-56478-853-5 (pbk. : alk. paper)
I. Title.
PQ2702.R42V5513 2013
843'.92--dc23
2013007219

Partially funded by a grant from the Illinois Arts Council, a state agency

Cet ouvrage a bénéficié du soutien des Programmes d'aide à la publication de Cultures-france/Ministère français des affaires étrangères et européennes

This work, published as part of a program of aid for publication, received support from CulturesFrance and the French Ministry of Foreign Affairs

www.dalkeyarchive.com

Cover: design and composition by Mikhail Iliatov

Printed on permanent/durable acid-free paper

VILLA BUNKER

by

Sébastien Brebel

Translated by

Andrew Wilson

DALKEY ARCHIVE PRESS

CHAMPAIGN / LONDON / DUBLIN

1. Perched on a cliff above the sea, looming and hostile, secretly opposed to anyone staying is what she'd written about the villa.

2. We see a house and we know immediately what sort of life is possible there. We contemplate its façade for a few minutes, we don't need to think rationally, nor linger before this unfamiliar house, she'd also written (in her chaotic and crude handwriting, full of careless and ill-formed letters). It takes less than a minute to understand everything. If we're going to be happy and lead an idyllic existence in this house, we already know it. If we're going to be unhappy and have a miserable life there, we know that as well, just as surely, just as quickly. We know right away if we'll be able to live in this house, or instead if we'll be forced to abandon the idea of living there. Its fitness or unfitness for habitation is immediately apparent. Everything we'll experience, everything we'll think and feel there, we can see it already as though we'd already lived it. In a matter of seconds, we can imagine our entire future existence in this house, we can see this life in minute detail and contemplate it as though it were over

and done with. This perception (she'd written) constitutes for us a truth, a certainty that will never be refuted, that we can't seem to get out of our heads. We imagine our possible lives in strange houses and, in the end, these existences pile up, one upon the other, somewhere deep inside us.

3. She turned on a faucet. The water, which was likely contaminated or poisoned by years spent in rusty pipes (she thought), ran red for several minutes. She'd made several trips to the supermarket during the day to stock up on cases of mineral water, now stored under the stairs.

4. She'd often stopped in the street to stare at the façades of houses, trying to imagine what life she'd lead inside; in the past she'd wondered many times while contemplating the front of an unfamiliar house: What would I have become if I'd had to live between those walls, what would I be thinking right now if I wasn't here in the street but rather on the other side, enclosed in one of those rooms? She would stop in front of expensive houses, it's true, but she was just as likely to stare at ugly, poorly maintained ones; in truth, she was liable to engage in this imaginary exercise in front of virtually any house. Now she couldn't take her eyes off the façade, she was counting the windows, calculating the number of rooms, she was imagining the wallpaper motifs, trying to perceive as many things as possible without getting any closer. Sometimes she would hear a musical instrument, she would listen to the sound of a piano and quickly gauge the ability

of the person playing; she would guess all kinds of things about the house's occupants. Some façades were alarming and would bring thoughts of misfortune to mind. She would perceive the noxious character of these sordid dwellings immediately, picturing her own life there, under a pall of sadness and boredom; she would see her possible life as an empty succession of dark and dismal days.

5. We are in a kitchen with peeling paint on the walls, condensation on the windowpanes obstructs our view of the outside. The yellow light of the florescent bulb above the sink, the dripping faucet, the mop on the floor, so many details assaulting us in this kitchen smelling of disinfectant and boiled meat. The conversations next door, the noise of the trays and the scraping sound of chairs being moved. The words they speak seem so strident, so oddly chosen, they make our heads spin. And long afterward, condensation still lingers on the windowpanes, and gives only a hint of the grounds beyond. We don't know how this is possible. Time has passed, we're not sure how much, we know that, in a way, the time spent in the kitchen doesn't count, we know of no measuring device capable of accounting for this time. We move to make sure we're still alive, but if we leave this room all these sensations might collapse, no longer having anything to refer to, and then we will have to devise other thoughts, form an entire system of new thoughts in order to continue.

6. And in that same street, when we happen to glance at a stranger, we sense that stranger's personality immediately, we sense his moods, his qualities and faults; he doesn't stay strange for long, this creature. It's enough to glance at him and his soul will open like a book, revealing the truth to us; now we know everything about him and are immediately in a position to judge the possible interactions we might have with this being, the kinds of relations we might maintain with him. If these relations are likely to turn ugly, become dangerous or simply intolerable, we know it immediately; we instinctively know we must avoid, even flee this potentially noxious being. There's no point striking up a conversation with someone we dislike at first sight, any such conversation will always be disappointing and sterile; actually, there's no point in having any kind of relationship with such a being, for it will be torturous from the outset, a shipwreck. When it comes to those supposedly enigmatic and secret entities (our fellow creatures), the secret is there's no secret at all. We penetrate at a glance the murky depths of such beings, their supposedly inviolable interiors. Before even speaking with them, we break into their interiority and we know everything about them, the real nature of their thoughts and desires, the fundamental reasons for their actions, their unspeakable dreams. We penetrate to the core of such beings, floating unsuspected in their interiority; there, we move through vacant fortresses like flying saucers in space.

7. The villa's front was completely without ornament, bare like a prison gate. The architect who had drawn up the exterior plan had certainly demonstrated his implacable hatred of ornamentation, systematically eliminating anything that

could've been mistaken for aesthetic ambition. Every façade is a statement, the front of every house a conscious intention. It was impossible to mistake it for something accidental, innocent, is what she'd written. And a façade like that is hard to take when it's without the slightest hint of decoration, or so she'd thought while standing next to my father. They were there in front of the villa, they hadn't said anything for quite some time, captivated by the sight of it. They were probably searching for something to say, though they were sure there were no words to describe what they were feeling. My parents were standing silent in front of the villa, sheltered under the umbrella my mother was holding in her hand (it was raining constantly and, eventually, her arm would go numb); they were contemplating the façade as though it were a sinister painting depicting their life to come. At that moment, they weren't sure what to think, it was as though their will was caught in an invisible net; perhaps they felt secretly attracted to this picture before them, as they measured for the first time the degree to which their life together had been determined by fate. Tired from the car ride, which had taken longer than expected, they had trouble concealing their reluctance as they turned down the uneven path. Everything about the façade's design seemed the product of an ill-will, inexplicably opposed to even the mere suggestion of luxury or comfort, so she'd thought glimpsing the façade through the windows of the car as it crawled slowly, like a hearse, down the gravel path, lined on both sides by overgrown hedges—this path had given her the feeling she was traveling down a long narrow corridor leading toward death. In a sense, the façade was something of an architectural feat, she'd said (or, rather, written) later while trying to recall her first impressions. Every line of thought began to aspire to its own erasure at the mere sight of this façade. The words "lugubrious" and "cold" had come to mind, and she was struck again by her inability to convey her exact impression. According to her, "lugubrious" and "cold" were too weak, they'd quickly become engulfed in a torrent of contradictory reevaluations. She'd experienced, she said, the limits of language, had foreseen her future wretchedness.

8. A seaside villa, though the use of the expression made you wonder. It would have been more accurate to speak of a former prison, or an abandoned one, she'd added (in writing), and she'd gone on to say that the impregnability of the place was an illusion. Locked bars on the first floor and cellar windows, windows partially barricaded with boards and corrugated metal sheets, she saw these as an apt expression of a feeling she couldn't otherwise have articulated. The bars had been put there as a precaution, my mother had said, in order to stop someone from breaking into the villa, yet in her mind this preventative measure had become punitive, designed to prevent anyone from ever leaving the villa, no matter what their reasons.

9. None of the other villas on the coastline had such a sinister appearance. Moreover, there weren't any other buildings visible in the surrounding area; the villa seemed completely isolated, cut off from the world, cut off even from those passersby who might discover it there, on the edge of the cliff, at a bend in the pebbly path. My mother had interpreted the villa's location, on the outer edges of the world, as yet another reason to despair.

10.
She was never able to rid herself of this image of a prison, or forget its walls blackened by dripping rain. And yet she'd tried everything to efface this unpleasant notion, dressing the façade in multiple ways so as to dissolve or bury it. In her imagination, she'd superimposed the geometry of a chalet, of an Indian pavilion, of a Norman manor on the villa, without ever managing to effect a lasting change in her impression of the façade. The mask was crumbling and would soon fall, then the prison façade would resurface again. Her first impression was reasserting its rights; underneath the rubble of the chalet, the pavilion, and the manor, the villa was being put back together, darker and more alarming than ever.

11.
We are worn down by dread, standing in front of the villa, as well as by the effort it takes to conceal this dread from ourselves, my mother had said; we are struck by the idea that people lived for years in the villa as recluses, and that we're soon going to take their place. Standing in front of the villa, my mother's first impression had been one of sudden hopelessness, brought on by the realization that they would soon be going inside. She'd begun to feel a senseless compassion for those who had stayed in the villa, and she'd even thought, absurdly, that someone might still be trapped inside, before realizing that this was just a new way to feel sorry for herself. But the villa was definitely theirs, theirs alone, and they would soon be living there, there was no way around it, that's what she'd told herself. For years they'd lived, comfortable and oblivious, never suspecting that someday they would find themselves here, in this precise place, on that cliff exposed to the wind, staring at that sinister

façade. They hadn't yet been inside, and frankly they knew next to nothing about the villa, about its atmosphere, but it had dawned on my mother that they would both be the villa's prisoners as soon as they crossed the threshold. She'd tried to fight this vague uneasiness, or at least keep it from my father by attributing her apprehension to fatigue and the nervous tension brought on by the car trip. And yet your father had seemed happy, all at once, when he first saw the villa, she'd said. Even though he was desperately trying to hide his excitement, his face had let a whole host of positive emotions float to its surface; these were so powerful that he even seemed younger. He'd been wholly won over by the look of the villa, she'd thought while observing these subtle, rapid variations in his demeanor, which resembled little nervous earthquakes. That day, she'd shown amazing docility. And in the following days she'd tried to get over her apprehension, showing unusual patience, as much to fool my father as to conceal her anxiety from herself. She'd gone outside numerous times to look at the front of the villa, and each time she'd run into the same image of a penitentiary. Sometimes she'd lock herself in the car and listen to Mahler's *1st* over and over again, she would watch the sea through the windshield while my father was wandering through the bedrooms, down the halls. The wind would whistle around her and the car seemed about to take off, ready to be lifted and carried away like some insignificant object. She could just make out the ghostly shape of a fishing boat in the far off distance, then her thoughts returned to him, he was floating through another world, or so she would think as she listened to Mahler, he didn't suspect a thing, but already he was no longer part of this world.

12. So she hadn't mentioned her apprehension, and she'd avoided talking about the villa at all in the days following their arrival, for fear of disappointing my father and setting off any sort of negative reaction. She had yet to utter the word "villa" aloud, she'd buried the word as deeply as possible, telling herself, as things stood now, it was best not to mention it, the word "villa" would never cross her lips again—instead, she acted as though they'd been living there for years, and really there wasn't much to say about it. Given their present situation, however, she'd decided it was best to warn me off: Above all, she wrote to me, I wasn't to try and see them, I was even to avoid seeing them, that is unless I was expressly invited. I must inform you of the potential risks you would run by visiting the villa, she wrote, which in its present state has every possible and imaginable problem, to the point of being considered inhospitable or even dangerous. Accidents happen so easily, my mother said.

13. I knew immediately, just by looking at the handwriting, that she wanted the letter to seem pathological.

14. The villa was uninhabitable, or so my mother kept saying, yet my parents had decided to stay there all the same, contrary to common sense, regardless of the risks; they'd moved all of their furniture, all their possessions, into a house lacking all comforts and seemingly ill-suited to them. So I wondered what could have gotten into my parents' heads to make them undertake the fatal project of living in a remote villa

isolated from everything, a house possibly about to collapse. The precise moment when our parents become strangers to us, just like the moment when we become perfectly inscrutable in their eyes, cannot be pinpointed, and we don't, by and large, even try. One day, we no longer recognize our parents, on one level we know these are our parents, yet we're still not quite convinced that our parents are actually these two beings who have become so unpredictable, uncanny, and try as we might to tell ourselves that our parents are perfectly free to do as they please, we begin to fear that they've embarked on a foolhardy, even suicidal course, and at every turn we worry that our fears will be realized. So we tell ourselves that we don't understand our parents at all, that we have long since ceased to make sense of their behavior, and that we can't even guess at the motives that lie behind their deeds—we watch our parents act, lamenting the arbitrary and absurd nature of their decisions. We begin to regard our parents as foreigners, indeed speaking to them as we would foreigners, employing words that seem borrowed from a tourist's phrase-book. Wouldn't it just be simpler and more sensible to let our parents do what they want? (We wonder about that, but then we realize we don't actually want to hear another word about them, we tell ourselves it would be best to remain oblivious to as much as possible.) Do our parents show us their true selves, we wonder; did we ever really know them? We witness the moment when our parents decide to undertake some catastrophic project, and we understand that realizing this project is absolutely vital and imperative in their eyes; and yet we wonder, why did it take so long for them to embark upon this plan? We talk to our parents about Derrida and Foucault, names they're familiar with since we've discussed them thousands of times, we want to make sure that our parents are actually the same beings with whom we have so often in the past discussed Derrida and Fou-cault—we can see, however, that these names no longer ring any bells. We have the feeling we're speaking in a strange, foreign language; our parents listen politely, but they don't understand, they look at us the way foreigners would, silent and impassive, they're simply waiting for us to finish talking about Derrida and Foucault—that is what we read on their faces. We try to imagine our parents on the cliff, but, really, no, we can't bring ourselves to believe it, we absolutely can't wrap our heads around the idea that they bought this villa perched on a precipice. We try again, this time endeavoring to imagine what their new life in the villa must be like, we imagine them eating meals in the villa, wonder-ing, for example, if they eat at a set time, or if they talk to each other at the table—indeed, it's been a long time since we've seen our parents eat. We make our parents act out all kinds of domes-tic scenes, in hopes of picturing for ourselves their new life, but in doing so we only become more aware of the distance between our parents and ourselves, and we sense we'll never be able to bridge this gap that separates us from them. It's impossible to know when we stopped feeling close to our parents, or at what decisive moment they began to seem strange to us, undoubtedly this distance has been developing for a long time, but we were too weak or too cowardly to notice it. As children, we're con-nected to our parents through love, and then one day we lose this emotional tie, we understand nothing when it comes to our parents and our childhood suddenly seems incomprehensible to us. It's impossible to bridge the gap that separates us from our childhood; once in place, this separation seems permanent and irreversible, and we have given up hope of overcoming it. We remember that we were once children, and when we recall this child that we once were, nothing about him makes any sense, he has now become a little stranger; we feel removed from this child whom we mentally dispatch to his own solitude, and in this way we take part in the disappearance of our own childhood.

15. They inspected the second floor, slowly traveling the length of the hallways leading to the various bedrooms. Isolated from the other rooms by these narrow corridors in which my parents were always getting lost, each room formed a kind of islet one could enter from different directions. Had the architect responsible for this layout wished to create a private space in each room, a sealed off accommodation where one could feel completely isolated? Yet another architectural detail that did not slip their notice: Depending on its location, each bedroom had a different number of doors, ranging from two to four. For example, each corner bedroom was accessible by two doors, whereas the four middle rooms each had three. The master bedroom was devoid of windows and had four doors. At first glance, the bedrooms all seemed modeled on the same plan: They had the same dimensions and were each completely vacant. As my parents entered each room, they were immediately overcome by a dusty smell, the air they breathed got stuck in their throats, the way air does when it has been shut up for a long time, and it seemed to have a pharmaceutical odor, further highlighting its impurity. They decided, nonetheless, not to air these rooms out, because the dilapidated windows, their chipped paint eaten away by humidity, were on the verge of collapsing. In every room, a light exhausted from making its way through dirty windowpanes prevailed over the clinical whiteness of the early morning, my

mother said. They detected, on the faded wallpaper, come un-glued or torn in places, the outlines of furniture and, likewise, the places where paintings had once hung. They inspected these walls without saying a word, contemplating for several minutes the dark spots on the floor, which were like elongated shadows at their feet. They couldn't gain access to the master bedroom, whose four doors were all locked. Because of the ever-present darkness in the corridor (they hadn't yet found the light switches), they circled this sealed-up room, feeling their way by following the cracks in the wall. They had the feeling they were circling a vault inside a bunker.

16. When they inspected the second floor again, the next day, to take more precise notes, nothing looked famil-iar. Everything now seemed much darker and more depressing than the day before. Had the look of the rooms changed in just a matter of hours? Despite their reluctance to admit these irregu-larities, they had to agree that the rooms gave rise to contradicto-ry impressions, so much at odds with their recollections from the day before that they were having trouble accepting that they were standing in the same place. Were these changes to be explained by the fact one could enter the same room via two or three different doors? They did, however, recognize the wallpaper motifs as well as other innocuous details: a small pile of dust carefully formed in the shape of a cone in the corner of one bedroom, a crack in the ceiling, the body of a fly mummified between two windowpanes, a cloth rolled around a doorknob. That's impossible, he said shak-ing his head. She wasn't sure she heard the sound of his voice so much as read the words on his lips, despite the poor light. He seemed to have forgotten she was there, inspecting the floors, walls, and ceiling with an unsettled look, going back and forth, his hands behind his back. They thought about the alterations of light and temperature, and later, comparing their impressions, they were tempted to attribute these sensory anomalies to subtle variations in their moods.

17. We have to consult the plans, my father said. That day he was speaking in a calm and delicate voice, though grimacing almost imperceptibly, my mother had noted. They were standing in the ballroom among the furniture and stacks of cardboard boxes, it was the first time he'd spoken to her directly since arriving.

18. They'd quickly decided to live in the ballroom. The first time they'd entered this space, my mother had felt she was walking into an airplane hangar rather than a room in a house, a huge deserted hangar big enough to house the burned-out husk of a warplane, she'd said. Every time I enter the room, I'm scared: It's so cold and formal, with high ceilings, and walls that seem to go on forever; it's hard for me to catch my breath in there, my mother said. Hundreds of people could easily have been put up in that one room, she'd remarked the first time she'd gone in; she'd felt lost in the midst of the vast vacant space, feeling like a mere passerby in the rubble of a city in ruin, a city leveled by bombs. I'd never seen a room that large before, or that austere, which was the sense I had of it, due to its dimensions

and absolute severity, my mother said; it could have housed a war machine capable of destroying an entire city. If the ballroom was beautiful, this too was due exclusively to its extraordinary coldness, its bareness. The question we ask ourselves when we enter this room is how long will we last, how long will we be able to stand the room's harsh chill. We've only just left the vestibule, and already we're in a war zone, and we think we hear the sounds of battle, all the while knowing that our senses are playing tricks on us, that we're dupes of an architectural illusion. As long as we're still in the vestibule, we don't suspect that, merely by pushing open the ballroom doors, we are going to find ourselves in the middle of a war, not for one second do we anticipate the sense of alarm hidden in the ballroom. The room's whitewashed walls are bare, there isn't the slightest ornamentation on these high walls, which, like the façade, have something merciless about them. On these chalk-white walls you can make out the places where large paintings must have hung for decades. The paintings are gone, but every time my mother's gaze happened to fall on one of those large faded rectangles, she would feel a pang of terrible anxiety, as though she had accidentally caught sight of something truly horrible. She would never learn what those giant ballroom canvases depicted, and anything she might imagine was no doubt far from being accurate; it was just that, judging from the space they took up on the walls, she was for some reason certain they could only have depicted horrific scenes, macabre settings. Perhaps they had been nothing more sinister than portraits of ancestors, but in that case, she was thinking, they're still big enough to give you the willies. She'd imagined a gallery of ancestors depicted as grotesque giants with monstrous heads measuring at least twice or three times the size of a normal human head, portraits of beings so excessive they'd lost all vestiges of human form. There, where others would have only seen the white surface of the walls, my mother could make out horrific heads in the spaces between the windows, heads hastily suggested with large brushstrokes against a background of garish, loud colors, invisible portraits she could nonetheless imagine and which, because she could not see them, had upon her an even more powerful effect.

19. Ever since their arrival, she'd felt like she was waiting for some climax to come.

20. She recalled how, on the first day, she'd immediately been frightened by the sound of the waves, a deafening roar that was impossible to escape. The villa seemed to have been built in the midst of the surf, battered on all sides, she said. A roar that was not only an aberration to the senses, my mother had added, it subjected thought to a constant and intolerable oppression. It was impossible to escape this incessant noise; in some parts of the villa, its volume could reach unimaginable proportions, a crashing sound that was not simply unbearable, it also prevented thought, inhibited concentration. She clearly had the sense the villa was built right in the middle of this noise; I often thought, my mother said, that the waves had laid siege to the villa, and now, living in constant fear of being swept away by the rising waters, my dreams have become dreadful, or rather nightmares. My mother would dream of the villa being swallowed by that mass of water, the millions of cubic meters of salt water bringing down the walls and carrying away the furniture, their possessions, carrying away their lifeless bodies like contorted mannequins, but when she awoke the terrifying noise would be gone; upon waking, I don't hear the slightest sound, I feel completely rested, as though I'd just slept fourteen hours straight, and I don't have to worry anymore, don't have to live in dread of a disaster; I feel much better in fact, almost relieved, writes my mother, I can imagine the villa is located in the middle of the desert, in the midst of a desolate landscape, out of reach, I can convince myself that the villa is in no way threatened by the waves; we're in the middle of nowhere, a barren expanse, sand stretches as far as the eye can see, and the silence is total; for days on end, the crashing sound disappears and a worrying silence, perhaps just as terribly heavy and oppressive, pervades the place in its absence. She dared not move an inch for fear of setting off the racket again, she remained at loose ends, incapable of finding anything to occupy her, or even sleep. Silence seemed to have taken possession of the villa once and for all, taken possession of their souls, but my mother couldn't help but wait for something to happen, a slight sound or occurrence, she'd written, that would break the spell and bring this hostile silence to a close. At first the silence had weighed on them like a cloak of concrete; eventually it would extinguish their recollections of what they had said to each other inside the villa. Soon she wasn't sure if she'd really heard the waves or if she had just imagined them; in the end she couldn't say for certain whether the villa was loud or quiet, whether it was pervaded by silence or exposed to the incessant roar of the waves; I wound up telling myself that the crashing of waves amounted to silence, my mother said. Such a silence, she'd come to understand, could only be explained by the fact that people who are subjected to a particular noise without respite eventually end up not even noticing it; they perceive as perfect silence what is in fact an unbearable racket.

21. Perhaps my mother had taken up writing in order to block out the noise, I thought, looking at her letter. I was holding it in my hand (it was the first time I'd ever received a letter from my mother), I'd carefully inspected the handwriting on the envelope, I was still looking at the letter itself; there was no need to read it to know what was inside, and I knew then I would be receiving more letters just like it, letters containing all sorts of information about my mother and the life she was leading in that villa, letters which would let me know how my parents were doing in their seaside retreat. She'd locked herself up in a remote bedroom, and in the privacy of this now-cherished room my mother was able to collect her thoughts as tranquilly as possible for her first letter. I was imagining her sitting in a chair, her head bent, her back ramrod straight, considering her words calmly before scribbling them on the page in her childish and crude handwriting, the handwriting of someone who hasn't written for ages, I thought at first, or rather that of someone who is afraid to write, and who at the same time feels the suppressed rage lurking behind all those signs on the page, signs that represent a kind of power in the process of being born; I could easily imagine her satisfaction with this, I knew that, from now on, she'd be hooked; with this thirst for a newfound power in words, she was going to find her way back whenever possible to the small, dimly lit room where she felt safe; there she would compose the rest of her letters, wrapped in the same silence, and she would again gauge the effect she might have, as though weighing her words upon some lunatic scale, perhaps even imagining my face as I read her sentences: She would see my expression, by turns annoyed and anxious, laughing at my confusion and concern as she continued to compose, still as absorbed and determined as ever, applying herself like a studious, stubborn schoolboy, yet still

incapable of quelling her nerves or controlling her actions—that's why she won't be able to stop her hand from scribbling more and more ungainly, more and more deformed words, words that will look, themselves, like bundles of nerves, metastases, then entire sentences written in a frenzy that will grow from the unreadable body of her text. The above is what I told myself later, turning the envelope over repeatedly in my hand, looking in turn at my hand, which was holding the envelope, and then at the envelope itself, as though I couldn't accept that both could be real at once.

22. Still, the ample dimensions of the ballroom had allowed them to store their furniture and all of their belongings on the first floor; they were able to set up headquarters in this one room alone, and right away. They'd figured initially that the renovations would only take a few weeks, which is why they thought it more practical to put all their furnishings in the ballroom, arranging the cardboard boxes in such a way as to create separate subspaces. However long the renovations take, they'd thought, they could easily camp out in the ballroom until the work was finished, without worrying about feeling cramped. Given its size, the ballroom could easily accommodate their furniture, as well as function as sitting room, bedroom, and kitchen, or anything else you might imagine, such were the practical if disturbing storage options provided by the room. So, from the start, they were no longer residing in a room, but rather a giant storage facility containing dozens of pieces of furniture, moving boxes full of clothes and other possessions, in short a warehouse whose capacity seemed endless. A ballroom that had originally been intended for receiving guests was transformed in a matter of

hours into a storage space stuffed with cardboard boxes; still, they never forgot their first impression of the room, and despite the familiar mess of oddly arranged furniture and boxes piled high, they retained this memory of a stately salon whose atmosphere was both cold and majestic. In the past, the gigantic chandelier hanging in the middle of the room had likely lit sumptuous furnishings arranged in a room meant for giving parties, a room that had once resonated with the sounds of Viennese waltzes, but at present this light was flooding down on our furniture in a jumble, and the dozens—or rather hundreds, my mother had quickly corrected herself—of cardboard boxes piled in the four corners of the vast room. I couldn't stop worrying that our stay in the ballroom, meant to be temporary, might drag on and on, my mother had written, that it could become permanent, that the sight of the boxes and oddly arranged furniture would become constant and immutable—in short, a depressing scene. All they had to do was look into the ballroom, she'd written, and in one glance they could see all their possessions gathered together as though for a still life. Everything we possess, everything we will possess, displayed in one place, all of it exposed to the eye as in a museum. The sight of their furniture, not to mention the various objects that had been removed from boxes and placed on the dusty floor, had more than once made her feel sick; she'd felt hemmed in on all sides, surrounded by the multitude of objects summing up their life together. She'd remarked that they'd have to find a place for it all, she'd have to think for hours in order to find the right spot for each object. She was there inside this loneliness, waiting gloomily among all these things that sent her back to their former life together, she held court in the midst of their property, striking a pose, both resolute and puzzled, as if on display herself, in an invisible case among those objects. She had a feeling she wouldn't be leaving the ballroom, she sensed she'd become a prisoner inside her own life.

23. My mother hid the fact she was writing these letters, not because she felt guilty about it, nor was she concerned about what my father would think if he found out (she'd never much cared about my father's opinion, nor about anyone else's for that matter), rather she'd always preferred deeds performed surreptitiously to those left in the light of day. My mother had always had a taste for secrets, and she'd always acted in the most secretive way possible, making of secrets a veritable religion, encouraging their cultivation whenever possible. And thanks to her, ever since I was a child, I shared this propensity for secrecy, this intractable, quasi-pathological compulsion; I grew up in a difficult and guilt-ridden environment, I was convinced that something, everything needed to be hidden, I too felt the need for secrets.

24. The individual characters on a page: just as wild as ever, as though they'd fallen or been dropped like bombs on the sheet of paper; that first letter almost looked like a devastated cemetery, with graves unearthed, crosses toppled.

25. And later, still not having read the letter, I wondered if I shouldn't tear it up, or at least stick it in a drawer

somewhere (just until I decided what to do with it); I could also have slipped it into a book taken at random from my shelf, that way putting off reading it until who knows when, but instead I weighed it in my hand again, an archeologist's careful gesture, as if I was holding a relic freshly exhumed from an Egyptian tomb. And honestly I couldn't even be sure the letter was addressed to me, and there was no way of knowing for sure, since the name written on the envelope was illegible and distorted, as if her hand had been trembling as she formed the letters, and I told myself my mother had been tempted, for some reason, to write another name in place of mine. For a long time I contemplated the jumpy edges of the letters, their rapid, uneven strokes, I guessed at the rage behind her movements, her relentlessness in writing to me, wondering if she was capable of faking such a frenzy, wondering whether my mother was at least aware that I was the one she was writing to—I couldn't even be sure of that. Well, she'd certainly written whatever name it was in a tormented and hostile script, one that acted immediately on my nerves, so in the end I decided that the name was my own.

26. Well, of course, I'd unsealed the envelope, I'd opened the letter, since I was convinced it was meant for me after all, but I'd still read the opening lines with a kind of superstitious mistrust, all the while wondering if I wasn't making a serious mistake, and I had the uneasy feeling I was myself acting somewhat suspiciously, as though I was guilty of something, I even had the nagging conscience of a guilty person. My heart pounding, I'd turned the pages, not daring to decipher what was written there, that's why I'd been careful to first remove my glass-

es, my myopia for once protecting me from the world, from its harshness, from its too precise contours, I'd skimmed the pages like a bomber on a reconnaissance mission, flying low over the devastated ground, but I'd noticed the letters scribbled on the page were getting larger, as if my mother had anticipated my ploy, as if, to annoy me, she'd wanted to drive her sentences into my head, and so now I had no choice but to read them: I was seeing the swollen sentences, feeling their hostility—they were like warnings, like alarm bells going off in my skull. I then said to myself, once they grow past a certain size, all words start to look like insults.

27. Has my mother figured out that my dissertation on Foucault is at a standstill, or does she think she's the only one fighting a losing battle? She didn't mention my dissertation in the letter, I know she'll never bring it up, she acts like it doesn't exist. I can't concentrate (I still haven't written the first word), but notes keep piling up on my table. I'm killing myself taking notes, rereading them, underlining and crossing out, yet the pointlessness of this busywork continues to haunt me. I bet she would be thrilled to see me like this, sitting at my desk, depressed and at loose ends, unable to write even a single line.

28. The degree to which these letters were a distraction from her boredom and loneliness, I couldn't guess; all I could figure out was, given the frequency with which they arrived, and their length, she'd found in them a favored and perhaps

necessary activity. In any event, a writing frenzy had clearly taken hold of her, and she'd given in to this epistolary penchant without the least hesitation. Each letter was supposed to describe the progress of the work being done on the villa, and the pages were indeed crawling with architectural details relating to the villa's renovation. She was utilizing the specialized vocabulary of architects and builders, and she often resorted to certain impenetrable terms of art, clearly getting great satisfaction from her use of such technical language. My mother included all kinds of superfluous details, she would pile into each letter a wealth of minutia in hopes of describing the villa as precisely as possible, but this only gave rise to more confusion.

29. The remodeling of the villa couldn't possibly start immediately. Such an undertaking, my father had said, required careful study and oversight, well in advance. Such an undertaking couldn't be taken lightly, without forethought; on the contrary, it demanded the utmost seriousness and a well-developed methodology. Several weeks, or indeed several months, were obviously needed to prepare for the work, several weeks or several months that would be entirely devoted to observation and reflection, in order to be sure the work got off on the right footing. If it's done in a hurry and without set guidelines, my father had said, it will all be doomed from day one. To start the work now, without having thought about it several weeks or even several months in advance, could be considered absurd, even suicidal. Generally speaking, my father had said, renovations like this are even more involved and daunting than building something from scratch—that's why remodeling can in no way be compared to

construction. We rush into a particular endeavor without being prepared for it, and we don't admit to ourselves that this endeavor demands from us a long period of preparation, and as a result we multiply the chances that our endeavor will fail. More often than not, we rush into something without really asking ourselves if we're capable of successfully completing it, without asking ourselves if we're up to the task. We buy a house, knowing full well that it doesn't suit us in its present state, but we have high hopes of fixing it up and furnishing it to our taste. We're going to redo everything (we think with the best intensions), transform everything, and immediately we come up with all kinds of plans, with the idea of furnishing this house and making it habitable. We have this house in front of us, but it isn't the house that we see, already we see another house just like the one we hope to be able to make. We project ourselves into the future without reflecting a single second on the likelihood of our actually realizing our plans, and more often than not we don't see the difficulties waiting for us in this future, and we don't suspect for an instant the obstacles that are about to keep us from realizing our plans. When we begin a certain project, we are more often than not optimistic, we tell ourselves it'll be easy to realize our plans, and we do everything we can to maintain this superficial optimism. Self-deception is the secret goal of every undertaking. From the beginning, we sense that we aren't up to the task and that we will be thwarted at every turn, but we want to remain oblivious, and so we charge ahead, throwing ourselves into our work in hopes of concealing our own doubts. And soon we will be forced to admit to ourselves: What a terrible idea, but we can't stop now, and we are forced to pay for the consequences of our haste. We say to ourselves: What an unbearable project, and what's worse, we've only just begun, we haven't even traveled a tenth of the way and all kinds of unavoidable obstacles and ordeals lie before us. From now on, our most cherished skill will be our ability to bear everything unbearable and hellish about our project without facing it head on, our entire lives devoted to concealing the absurd and disingenuous nature of our undertakings.

30. It's not so much that my mother found these comments ill-considered, only surprising coming from a person she'd known in the past to be taciturn, prudent, and skittish—yes, she'd lived for years with this being who simply exuded silence, putting up bulkheads of silence the way others wrap themselves in words, opinions, and rumors, someone who had turned silence into an art form, getting us all quite accustomed to life in his silent temple; for we all considered silence to be superior to words—you might say silence had become our preferred mode of communication—which is why she'd been shocked by this unprecedented profusion of words, and she immediately blamed it on the villa, immediately saw this as a sign of the villa's influence on his usual mode of thought, which is why she'd begun observing him (my father) more and more discreetly, spying on his reactions, following his reasoning, the way a lab technician would.

31. Again this morning, my mother writes, his voice is sounding so affected, I'm having trouble recognizing it. This voice is, however, clear and irrefutable, like the movement of the hands around the dial of the alarm clock sitting on

my bedside table.

32. My father's every sentence, and soon his every gesture, every movement, will be described and analyzed, and she's not going to spare me any of the details, I say to myself as I attempt to decipher her opening pages—and that's just for starters. In the future, she'll not only describe the progress made on the villa and their difficulties getting used to their new life, she'll also scrupulously record all these symptoms, from the faintest to the most flagrant, following their progression, or their decline, measuring, day by day, week after week, on a somewhat erratic curve, the changes affecting my father's personality. And I was inflicting each letter on myself as though it were a medical report, a medical report from which I gleaned absolutely nothing, I would read, I would swallow it all, without having the slightest idea what my parents were really going through, I would sink into a world of hearsay and antinomy, in which everything seemed falsified, improbable, secretly designed to ruin my life.

33. I would eventually come to see each letter as a kind of work of art, complete with their periodic bright points, vivid blue, their desert passages riddled with capitals. I would say to myself: My mother the artist; or else: My mother is going mad.

34. They were no longer using the word "villa," and related expressions like "villa on the coast" and "seaside villa" had disappeared from their vocabulary as well. One day we stop saying such and such a word, and having completely given up the use of this word, it drops out of our vocabulary entirely. We continue to talk, of course, finding ways to speak about anything in the villa as if nothing has changed. In the villa, my mother wrote, we never say the word "villa," and we weren't quite sure at first what was keeping us from saying it, it's just that, every time the word "villa" comes to mind, we instinctively get around it by saying "house" instead of the word "villa," which has now been banished and forbidden. The word "villa" is there somewhere in our brains, of course, most likely in a fairly remote part, getting more remote by the day, each passing hour only drives it farther away. Soon we won't need to remind ourselves that this word isn't to be uttered, and we'd be at a loss anyway to explain the unconscious mechanisms at work whenever we reject this term in favor of another—and, actually, we don't really know why this word has become taboo for us, but the simple fact is it never crosses our lips. For fear of my father's reaction, she'd begun to refrain from using the word "villa," and he'd done the same, without consulting her. Meanwhile, they continued to speak normally and on the surface nothing changed, as the days went by their voices played opposite one another in the villa. They would breathe, take their meals, remove their clothes, sleep, completing all sorts of tasks just as they would have anywhere else. And even though the word "villa" was no longer spoken, it continued to exist, and they found themselves in between its walls, two flesh-and-blood intruders moving about in a shadowy, secluded world to which they had forced entry. But now they could only designate this world by alluding to it, communicating in innuendo about a world each day more confused, more unstable, a world whose boundaries and contours were increasingly unclear.

35.

And I began to look forward to these letters, even though I knew they would end up annoying me and eventually make me sick. I was already well acquainted with their annihilating power. And how, hours after having read them, I was still in the grip of my mother's sentences, and for my part I couldn't write a single one of my own, I was unable to concentrate on anything, I was stuck with hers: sentences that sometimes seemed dictated by sluggishness, written in handwriting permeated by fatigue and boredom, while at other times they could be extremely elegant, filling my head with her hysteria; sentences that haunted me in dreams; they weren't so much words I was deciphering as obscure signs, individual letters, or things crossed out; sometimes they were only stains, sometimes insects, intermingled and frenetic hybrid beings whose monstrous marriages crawled across the page, denying themselves to my intellect—that's why I'd often get up in the middle of the night to reread the letters under my lamp's orangey arc light, as if to make sure I hadn't dreamed them; but no, I hadn't dreamed them up, nor were they the fruits of my imagination, but still I was having trouble focusing, and in the end all I could make out were formless little corpses, sticky and shriveled-up pieces of flesh bathed in orange light.

36. But at other times, I would hear this dark, dissonant music coming from nowhere, and it was as though I was reading in my mother's discordant notes the echo of some funeral march.

37. According to my father, the kind of thinking it took to renovate the villa wasn't something you could do just anywhere, everything had to be just right; what was required was a carefully selected place, or even an ideal place, he'd added for my mother's benefit. One day, they'd just shown up at the villa, without having the slightest idea how much time and effort would be required for its renovation. Their life had taken a decisive turn, they knew there was no turning back now—they knew the time for regrets was over. The day they'd arrived, they'd put all their furniture and other possessions into the vast ballroom on the first floor. They'd spent the following days sorting through a few things, opening and closing the cardboard boxes numbered with black marker, pushing the furniture this way and that—it was now essentially a furniture warehouse. They weren't sure how long they would have to stay in that part of the villa. They organized their new life with every intention of not giving in to the inevitable disappointment that comes with a task as immense as their own. They'd have to get used to camping among the wrapped-up armchairs, the shafts of rolled rugs, they'd have to learn to live with the crates and cardboard boxes piled high.

38. She couldn't even listen to Messiaen or Fauré anymore, she was no longer able to indulge her musical impulses in the villa—these habits were broken for good. She would glance distractedly at her sheet music, turning the pages as though leafing through a book she wasn't interested in. She would approach the piano. The movers had placed it in the middle of the ballroom, following my mother's precise instructions. For several minutes my mother would remain dumbfounded in front of the instrument, wrapped in its thick gray blankets. The piano on which my mother had played and replayed Bach, Fauré, and Messiaen resembled a wounded pachyderm, sentenced to silence beneath its dusty jacket.

39. The villa needed to be explored, each room paced back and forth in, every last corner rummaged through, in order to uncover that most propitious place for the work of thought.

40. So she'd gotten into the habit of constantly quoting my father in her letters, letters signed with her name yet filled with sentences not her own, sentences she would put on like clothes perfectly suited to her taste and style, thus sentences spoken by my father, which my mother would memorize, and then scrupulously transcribe as soon as she was alone again in that part of the villa where she'd found a semblance of peace and security. And when I read these letters, I couldn't be sure who their author was, of course I would recognize my mother's writing and try to imagine her bent over the page, as focused as ever, as though playing the piano (I often thought), but I'd still harbor doubts about the origin of those sentences written by her, what secret score was my mother composing (I wondered)—she had to be terribly lonely to have filled up all these pages.

41. The bedrooms weren't all vacant, though. In fact, as my mother and father worked their way through the upper floors, they noticed that the number of objects and pieces of furniture left behind increased with each story they climbed, as if the previous owners, forced to leave in a hurry, had given up on emptying out the rooms upstairs. This gave us the uncomfortable feeling we'd broken into the villa, my mother had said, as though we were somehow trespassing. The majority of the bedrooms on the third floor contained only one shabby piece of furniture in a sorry state: a chair, a mattress lying on the floor, a table filled with glasses and vials, that's all. They discovered neither photos nor traces of writing, there was no way of knowing anything specific about the bedrooms' prior occupants, instead you had the vague sense of walking through a dormitory, of visiting rooms in a boarding house. In one of the rooms they found only an armchair, arranged slightly askew next to a window; it seemed its occupant could retake his place at any moment and continue his daydreaming just where he'd left off before exiting the room. More troubling still for my mother was the taste of the objects, their style, and the way the general layout varied from room to room, as if the various parts of the villa bore no relation to one another. She'd even thought perhaps the villa had been home to several boarders, boarders whose tastes and preoccupations were

so different they'd all coexisted in complete indifference to one another, forming a kind of invisible community made up of disparate and singular parts, royally unaware of their fellow tenants, probably never speaking, communicating only through the unavoidable daily sounds of their mere presence. According to my father, the furniture and objects were without question part of the villa, it was impossible to distinguish between the villa and the things left inside it, which as a result now formed an integral part of the house—in certain respects, the house was already being lived in, or at least they would have to think of it that way for the time being. When we buy a house, and this house is not vacant as expected, we're well within our rights to consider that everything inside it now belongs to us, and as a result we have to get used to the idea that we are now the owners of all these possessions, we must think of these possessions as our own, reflecting calmly on how we might put them to use, without making any rash decisions.

42. At first glance, the layout of the bedrooms on the third floor followed a simpler plan, common to hotels and corporate apartments. The bedrooms facing north and south were situated on either side of a central corridor. The square footage, however, and even the height of the ceiling, seemed to vary noticeably from room to room, possibly an optical illusion due to the odd placement of the furniture, or the number and styles of the objects present. Still, as my mother and father went from room to room, they noticed differences of light and temperature so extreme as to give the impression the seasons had suddenly changed, they would get very hot and begin sweating only to be frozen from head to toe a few minutes later, they would shiver as though they'd just walked from summer to winter, their bodies subjected to harsh and unpredictable temperature fluctuations, and they said to each other that, in the future, they'd better bring a backpack with hats and sweaters and powerful flashlights.

43. They began to pay close attention to their own reactions, listening for their heartbeats when they entered a bedroom, paying attention to the way the light affected their retinas. Their eyes half-closed, they would always exchange a few brief comments, as though they were testing the acoustics.

44. Certain doors, which had been stuck closed the first time they went through the house, opened a week later with a simple push of a shoulder. All the doors in the attic were ajar.

45. After she learned of these furnished rooms, my mother was constantly on edge; she was now convinced she would never be able to live normally in this house that seemed to grow bigger by the day, a house so immense she could never recall just how many rooms it had. These rooms and their furniture were giving her a guilty conscience, she'd said, they were keeping her awake at night. She was convinced each room was conceived for a specific purpose, furnished and decorated for staging a particular drama at a given moment in the life of a being she would never meet. She would open a door and immediately be submerged in a hostile universe, at once cold and arbitrary. She would experience a feeling of isolation, as though she were locked in a ship's cabin, lost in the middle of the ocean. She would see a man's jacket on a chair, and this abandoned article of clothing would haunt her thoughts, this individual thing among so many others would dispossess her of herself; the old jacket would come to life in the silence of a bedroom (someone had left it there), and all around the chair things would stir, one by one, things roused from their sleep, awakened by her mere presence, she'd thought, and now these things wanted her to notice and recognize them. And when she was asleep, these inhabited spaces would go on frightening her, and she would dream she was in a bedroom surrounded by strange and ugly pieces of furniture. In this room, everything was green and cracked and yellow. She would sit at a small vanity, opening the flasks, inspecting the contents of the small boxes. She would look up and contemplate her image in the mirror. Behind her, an unmade bed that was not hers. And on the ground, at her feet, women's clothes covered the entire surface of the floor, forming a mosaic of multiple colors and fabrics, clothes that had been worn by someone no longer there and perhaps now dead. She was wondering why she'd scattered all these clothes on the floor, as she contemplated her work, speculating that she'd just committed some sort of sacrilege. She was wondering if these clothes might not be hers.

46. On the fourth and fifth floors, things got really complicated.

47. The plans left by the lawyer after they'd closed the sale were faulty, erroneous, even absurd. After having carefully examined them for hours, trying in vain to make a connection between the obscure indications found there and the actual layout of the villa, my father had destroyed these illegible plans, calling them architectural aberrations.

48. In a room on the top floor, abnormally small pieces of furniture, as though they'd shrunk, or were built for dwarves.

49. It was out of the question to store all that broken furniture, those out-of-order relics, in the basement. Chairs, jugs, broken dishes, empty suitcases, or rather suitcases filled with moth-eaten clothing—the basement was already full of rubbish from the past. A wheelchair, various canes, books swollen by humidity, old newspapers—the basement was so cluttered, so saturated with heavy and cumbersome prehistoric objects, it was virtually impossible to enter. She often said: It's all got to go, destroy it all, but he never so much as answered—it's possible he hadn't heard my mother's complaints, and was simply continuing his deliberations as though my mother hadn't said a thing. She would've liked to sell all the furniture; even better, she would've loved to throw it out the window, light a fire in the front yard, and watch everything disappear in flames. He wouldn't give her an answer, and she knew he would never allow the villa to be cleared out, he seemed attached to the furniture, convinced that they had to keep the villa just as they'd found it until the renovations could begin. Then, one day, he'd suggested they could make some money by selling the furniture, thus recouping part of the cost of the renovations, but he'd done nothing to make this happen, and would do nothing until he was done correcting the blueprints—this she'd known full well, she would have to get used to the furniture, get used to living in those dreary surroundings. In the meantime, my father was against altering the arrangement of the furniture, forbidding my mother to touch anything, he wasn't even going to let her take down the wallpaper, he was issuing all sorts of diktats to which she would grudgingly submit. Everything is to stay exactly where it is. For months, maybe for years, my mother thought, the villa would remain exactly as it was, and they would do nothing to change it; on the contrary, they would do everything in their power to maintain the villa in the state in which they'd found it, being careful not to alter whatever it might be, attenuating by any means possible the effects of their presence, erasing their tracks as if to stop time.

50.

They had to repeat their inspections of the villa to get their bearings and familiarize themselves with the place. These successive and painfully slow trips had taken on a disturbing, exploratory quality. Each time, my parents would discover a new aspect of the villa, and a detail that had previously escaped their notice would suddenly spark their imagination. One day they were uncovering a hidden door that opened onto a string of strangely small rooms, the next they were discovering a tiny staircase that apparently led nowhere. They would try in vain to explain these anomalies, they were beginning to doubt the evidence of their senses, or they would blame their faulty memory. A crack detected in the ceiling of a bedroom, whose walls they'd already measured and carefully examined, could plunge them into deep confusion. Surrounded in sudden darkness at the end of a corridor, they would bump into a piece of furniture, trip over a broken object, and they would remark to each other that this object hadn't been there the last time, each blaming the other for having moved it. They had to take along a flashlight in order to make their way through the parts of the villa that were without electricity. The extra batteries in my parent's pockets reassured them, they would say to each other that they couldn't get lost in the poorly lit villa, they had a light source and hours of battery life left. But in the darker areas, where it seemed the air was thinner, they still proceeded cautiously, feeling their way with their free hands. The poor state of the floors and windows, the strange changes in light from one room to the next, they smelled a trap at every turn. Even after having lived there for several weeks, they still felt as though they were wandering around inside a house no more familiar than on the first day; the house seemed more hostile with each passing night, and inside it they themselves felt like two perfect strangers.

51. He would come and go in the villa the way thoughts come and go in an overworked brain, she said. She accompanied him sometimes, when he would ask her to. Was he afraid of getting lost? He took the same hallways, climbed the same stairs several times a day. They were two characters in a silent film, making uncertain, jerky movements, as though they were walking the deck of a boat in a storm. They would enter tiny

rooms that would seem to contract even further around them, and their hearts would begin to race; they would rapidly inspect the walls while holding their breath, exiting again one or two minutes later, exhausted. There was intense cogitation going on in my father's head, my mother had written, the gears were spinning, and she could tell that he was agitated. Jogging behind, she'd follow his outline through the corridors. She could see his thoughts just by looking at him from behind. They were racing through his head, she would say, each thought bumping into and nipping at the one before it, separated only by a thin partition.

52. His slight smile as he poured the contents of an aspirin packet into a glass of water told her of his strange happiness. In moments like these, he seemed to get a mysterious pleasure out of lauding his own incomprehension.

53. They were growing apart little by little, irresistibly, they almost never spoke to one another anymore, exchanging useless and empty comments when they did, and at first she was tempted to attribute this distance to the size of the villa, a house that was too big for them, she often thought, and which was keeping them from communicating normally, from living normally. Only when we know each room, and can situate it in relation to the other rooms, can we then inhabit a house, not before, my mother had said. When we don't know how many rooms a house contains, inhabiting it is humanly impossible, living in such a house would soon make you sick. The sad state of

the villa was making their stay more difficult, the villa was show-ing all the signs of being unsound, and in its present condition it had all the features, all the drawbacks of a vacant and condemned building. She'd imagined all kinds of potential accidents, due to the poor condition of the floors in certain rooms, and the lack of adequate lighting. She was afraid of getting lost, but it would be even worse to sprain her ankle or fall to her death in a stairwell—that's why she'd restricted her movements to certain areas inside the house. But seeing as this decay had been at work for years, the villa was unlikely to be fazed by mere human attempts to refurbish it (that is what she was telling herself): It would remain an inhospitable and uninhabitable villa until the bitter end, no matter what their attempts to renovate it and make it to their liking, or simply better suited to their needs. She'd often thought of those elated home owners who end up hanging themselves from a metal beam, men and women who had lived for years with the dust, surrounded by rubble and plastic tarps, people who had done the rounds of all the banks and building contractors, and who in the end gave up on living in this house, which had closed in upon them like a carnivorous plant, sucking away their strength, killing their hopes—the following words could often be found in their pockets, on notes scribbled by way of apology: We hate this house (words they'd screamed in their heads hundreds of times before the end of their days).

54. Various alterations in my father's physiognomy: At times he seems extraordinarily old, at others extreme-ly juvenile. His wrinkles seemed to disappear, then reappear, and even his skin tone apparently changed as he made his way

through the house. Like a surface sensitive to the influences of its environment, sensitive to the subtle variations of temperature and light in the rooms and corridors through which he wandered without purpose, my father's changing face seemed to fall prey to this erratic weather. My mother used to stare at that climatic face of his, thwarted in her efforts to arrest its image in her memory.

55. She'd examined the clothes she found, turning over the collars in hopes of reading a name there, or finding a clue, which might have finally settled the matter.

56. It was as though the villa were growing, expanding gradually, constantly. The rooms were multiplying, forming something like a long snakelike dwelling space, whose coils extended over several floors. My mother and father were still getting lost, and their almost daily forays weren't exactly helping, the villa was like a Chinese puzzle, my mother said, an unsolvable puzzle whose pieces refused to fit together, a game of patience seriously testing their nerves, forcing them to go around and around in circles. You should have seen them, my mother scurrying after my father (he'd picked up the pace on their daily trips). The more they inspected the villa, the more difficulty they had finding their way and getting their bearings. At any moment they could feel as though they were in the middle of nowhere, even when they were in the ballroom. But the dread was even worse when it would catch them alone, by surprise. My mother would try to concentrate on a book and suddenly she would become giddy at the thought that the room she was in was separate, isolated from the other rooms; she would have to go see for herself, she would turn the doorknob, darting a nervous glance outside, as though she were expecting to find herself on the edge of a cliff. If you ask me, they were victims of an architectural curse.

57. He was moving faster and faster, barreling down the hallways, opening and closing the doors, giving the rooms a quick once over, estimating at a glance the size of the bedrooms, length and breadth of the corridors, the height of the ceilings and steepness of the stairs, the incidence of light at this or that time of day, and the consequences thereof. And after nightfall, when he was about to fall asleep, new doors would open in his brain; he would climb stairs in his head, visiting the bedrooms one by one in a depressingly predictable order, inspecting his memories the way one mechanically shuffles a deck of cards, double checking the placement and size of each room, all the while still wandering through his dream villa, as though it were the backdrop for a play.

58. The relative placement of the furniture, the arrangement of a table and chairs, the number of armchairs and the incline of their backs, the amount of space between the shelves, faded rectangles left behind by paintings now taken down; the precarious arrangement of objects, flasks around the sink, makeshift knickknacks on makeshift sideboards and end tables, a pink rubber glove partially turned inside out on the rim

of the tub. My father had spontaneously begun taking notes in a small notebook that he'd carry around with him everywhere. At his request, my mother would aim the flashlight at the point of his pencil, all the while trying in vain to make out his jumbled writing. What use did he hope to make of these annotations?

59. They would hear noises coming from upstairs. Sometimes the villa was like someone sleeping, someone who might twitch a few times in the night, trying to wake up, but who then falls back asleep.

60. He'd begun to mistrust his memory. He was convinced the villa was changing each day, taking advantage of their time asleep, or even a moment's distraction, to give birth to a new room, or to alter the layout of the premises. He would enter a room through one door one day, only to discover another door to the same room the following day, and this change in perspective would make him think he was in a different room entirely. He would inspect the walls, check the height of the ceiling, contrast the variations of light "here" as opposed to "there." The rooms in the villa were like memories, he'd commented. When each time we remember something, we take a different path to it each time we recall it, and in this way each memory ends up eventually leading us to the same thing—but at the same time each new memory makes the journey longer.

61. There was a simpler explanation, however. They'd noticed that walls had been put up all over the place, probably in an attempt to partition the space of the villa into more rooms by making each individual room smaller. These walls—which had leaped up everywhere, to excess, subdividing the existing rooms—had systematically altered the dimensions of the living space, so as to make it (by accident or design) uninhabitable. It was no surprise that the overall plan of the villa seemed so complicated. Moreover, these new walls made it difficult to access certain rooms. This architectural aberration, my father had said, could only be the product of a sick mind. The man responsible for these walls had likely suffered from some pathological need for isolation.

62. Or perhaps he was a psychologist who liked observing the behavior of rats in a maze.

63. They would sometimes have to go through several windowless adjoining rooms, rooms which were like cells in a prison or an asylum, before finding daylight again. In these rooms light was provided by rudimentary fixtures at best, probably not up to code. And when they would flick the switch, a bare bulb would spill harsh light on their heads. Frayed extension cords ran along baseboards with chipped paint.

64. It seemed the journey would never end.

65. Were his senses playing tricks on him, when he would enter a bedroom and recognize the furniture, was he really standing in the bedroom he thought he was in, as he calculated the square footage and rearranged the furniture in his head; had he really perceived something when he knew full well that come evening he wouldn't be able to locate this room again, nor recall through which corridor he'd traveled to get there? Come evening, he would have trouble saying if the room existed at all.

66. She'd recognized the camera immediately, an old model that she'd thought lost or broken. And it'd actually looked like a makeshift toy, completely ridiculous, my mother said, the strip of tape wound around the base of the lens had only added to the sense that it would never take a clear picture. The camera, she'd said, had hardly looked like a real camera, but instead was like a crude copy, completely lacking the qualities required of a piece of photographic equipment—that's why at first she'd thought my father wasn't really going to take pictures, but instead was only playing a trick on her. Seeing the camera, my mother had winced; she remembered my father taking pictures, remembered how manic he had gotten, in the old days, bringing out his camera at the slightest instigation, in order to capture this or that scene. She'd seen his face from long ago, that sweet and frantic face he made while adjusting the lens, and she'd re-

membered how posing for his shots always took forever. He used to take dozens of portraits of her, giving her directions, how she should stand, what expression she should have, he would speak to her as though she were a model, and he a professional photographer, giving her added direction and suggestions so the picture would be perfect, but in the end all he ever got out of her in these sessions was irritation. She would tell him she was through with these shoots, shoots that she found as grotesque as they were exhausting; she would declare—as she had so many times before—that she didn't want to be his model anymore, that he could just go get himself a professional model if the photos weren't to his liking, yes, and while he was at it he could find somewhere else to practice his talents, too—that's what she would repeatedly tell him, all the while posing, that is until my father finally had to give up photographing her, abandoning portraiture for landscape photography, but my father wasn't deterred, far from it, he'd started taking even more photos now that he was free to train his lens on the motif of his choosing. Every detail was apparently worth his trouble, every situation deserving of immortalization in my father's eyes. Absolutely anything would find favor in his photographer's gaze, some small detail that would've appeared banal or pointless to anyone else constituted for him something worthy of being locked inside the camera obscura. For my father, the visible world was a warehouse of images, images of things that he had to capture, as though to make sure that these things really existed—at least that's what I think now. Truth is, my mother had never been able to stand the constant presence of his camera, and she'd gotten in the habit of systematically objecting whenever my father would point the lens in her direction—purely formal objections, I often thought. My mother used to hate to have her picture taken, in any case that's what she would always maintain—and I thought about all the times my mother had tried to flee the lens with a wave of her hand, and all these times made up a single image of her, a photograph of my mother pushing the lens away with her hand, an image that's engraved in my memory, I thought, and which exists only there. And when faced with the camera that had been missing for years, now suddenly resurfaced and in my father's hands, thinking back to all those useless photos my father had taken of us, my mother could only have put her hand in front of her face again, instinctively obeying the irresistible and irate impulse lying intact inside her; yes, twenty years after the fact, how could she have done otherwise, my mother had once again escaped the lens, I told myself, and the photo would again be blurry.

67. In the villa, my father could again devote himself to his passion, a passion that had remained intact all these years, and perhaps had even grown stronger, I imagined, owing to the simple fact that he'd completely stopped taking pictures in the intervening years; for some reason unbeknownst to my mother, he'd one day put the camera away, downgrading it to the category of useless objects that one keeps without knowing why. But now, armed with the camera again, he'd even given up his diligent inspections; he was apparently so engrossed in taking pictures that he'd completely forgotten about the renovation project. Like a weary tourist lost inside his own home, my mother had said, he would turn the camera in various directions, as one might an optical instrument, a second organ of sight capable of letting him see what his own eyes could not.

68. He hadn't lost his knack for taking the same picture again and again, always from the same angle, photos that only he could tell apart, once they were developed and arranged on a table so he could examine them closely. Each week, he would entrust my mother with several rolls of film, which she would take to the express lab in the shopping center where she bought groceries. Each week, she would wander the aisles of the grocery store, mechanically filling the basket while she waited for the photos to be ready.

69. Was he planning to reconstruct a comprehensive view of the villa by gluing dozens of photos end to end? It's quite possible he'd had this project in mind in the beginning, my mother said, but he must have given up on it later, pointing the lens at random, photographing almost without discrimination, without method, zooming in on a detail, tracking the smallest clue liable to put him on the path to a new discovery. During this same period, he'd brought out the old photo albums, and he would often talk to her about these family photos, carefully examining each one. The older we get, the dearer these photos are to us, he would say as he slowly turned the pages, as though they were the pages of some rare and precious book; in our eyes, these photos are worth more than the most precious work of art, they are our works of art, the only works that matter to us. One day we begin to doubt our memories, we realize that our memory is faulty and that most of what we remember is distorted, and since our memory is flawed, we decide to reject outright everything we remember, relying instead on photographs, which have become in our eyes the only true memories; we consult these photographic images more and more frequently, and by examining these photos in the light of our critical judgment, we forget our own memories—that's why we're so attached to photos of ourselves as children, and to ones of our parents, but we're also just as attached to other family photos, and in a general way to every photo in our possession. It's not unusual to find, among these family photos, pictures of people we can't identify, beings we can't name and who are strangers to us. We've glued their photos to the album's pages, next to the other photos, and soon, after contemplating their image, we get to know these beings, who wind up almost becoming part of our family. A photo of a perfect stranger can make us think we know and understand this stranger's personality, as though we had a relationship with the person depicted in this photograph. We come across a picture of a stranger and we are immediately engrossed and caught up in this stranger's world, we begin to have a certain feeling about him, and we act as though we know this being from a prior period in our existence. Once we've looked at this photo carefully and immersed ourselves in it, we can no longer forget it, we don't know who took this photo, and we don't have any information about the person in it, we examine his clothes, relying upon their style to date the photograph, and more often than not we can't even manage to track down the stranger's name. This stranger's name and personality have been erased, all that's left is his image in an old snapshot, which we consider without being able to look away—and frankly we can no longer feel indifferent to this photo. The stranger in the photo can smile all he wants, but we aren't fooled by this smile, we grasp right away that this stranger feels an infinite sadness; in a flash of insight, we get in touch with the stranger and read his thoughts as though in a book. So it's impossible for us to destroy a photo like this, even when it's out of focus and hasn't come out right—that is the one sacrilege we refuse to commit. Destroying this photo would amount to a serious affront to the person found in the picture, it would be like a crime committed against this unknown person who has become in our eyes strangely familiar. And when all is said and done—after we have stared at these photos of some stranger or another—we turn our attention back to the photos of our parents, and we tell ourselves that they're the ones who have become strangers, they're the ones we now don't recognize and who seem distant and strange. I realize the photos are of my parents, but I also realize that what I am looking at is not my parents, but rather actors or extras who merely resemble them; these people have put on my parents' clothes and are simply imitating my parents' gestures. And try as they might to look just like them, they aren't my parents anymore, they are instead fictional characters with the grace and composure of immortal beings, they are two inaccessible beings striking a pose for eternity.

70. By chance, she found one of the first snapshots of the villa on the floor, slid under a bedroom door. Had the photo fallen out of his pocket, or had he left it there intentionally? The photo reminded her of a bookmark left inside an old tome. It was, in my mother's exact words, the first clear sign of an illness that had taken years to develop.

71. So that in a couple of weeks, shots of the villa were piling up more or less everywhere. She used to find

some on the ground, discarded, others tacked to the walls, on the doors. Interior shots in which she would recognize a bedroom, a bird's-eye view from the top of the stairs. The photos quickly spread, like a disease. There were probably even more in the room at the top of the tower, she thought. The room must have been chock-full of photos, underexposed shots, crossed out, stained, strewn upon the floor, photographs arranged like tarot cards on the camping cot, she thought. She used to imagine my father leaning over the bed, examining each photo carefully as though with a magnifying glass, pointing to a detail, running his finger one way and then the other over each row of photos, as though trying to find the key to an enigma. The photos became stained and ruined. He used to sleep on them sometimes. He also used to wedge them under tables and chairs. And when a photo found favor with him, among the hundreds neglected and forgotten, he would glue it to a piece of cardboard, sometimes sketching in a frame around it with a ballpoint pen.

72. But far from offering a stable, definitive image, something he could hold onto and store, the photos were having the opposite effect. Shot from every angle, the villa had seemed to fall to pieces, scattering to the four winds, lost beneath its infinite contours. It's like the villa's getting away from us a second time, my mother said.

73. These fits, these bouts of illness were getting worse; they'd intensified during the course of their stay and

had ended up becoming quite pronounced, first as isolated symptoms and then as outright illness, even grave illness.

74. One day, when he was by himself in a bedroom on the third floor, opening a dilapidated armoire, he'd discovered the spiral staircase. The armoire (an antique) was likely to contain old, moth-eaten clothes, he'd thought, damp rough sheets; he has no idea what made him open the armoire, he wasn't usually curious about the contents of old pieces of furniture, he was mostly content to look without touching, fearful that he would end up crushed under a rain of rubble and rotten planks. As a matter of fact, as he was opening the armoire's large doors, he'd felt a cool breeze on his face, as though he were standing at the entrance to a mine, in front of its shaft. He might well have never noticed this secret passageway leading directly to the top of the tower, he explained later to my mother (at the time he was in a state of extreme agitation), and for good reason, it wasn't just that the staircase was invisible, it didn't figure in any of the plans, plans he'd studied many times before destroying them. Why had someone concealed this staircase, what secret could they possibly be hiding, questions nagging inside my mother's head, while my father kept repeating that he'd found the ideal environment upstairs; my mother was unsure what he'd meant exactly by ideal environment (and she would probably never be sure)—she'd noticed my father's extreme agitation and wondered if it wouldn't be best to leave him to his ravings. She should go have a look, he would say, attempting to reassure her, speaking to her as to a frightened child—she couldn't possibly imagine the significance of the discovery as long as she refused to follow him up the stairs and see

for herself how the air up there was clean and pure. You win, she'd said, realizing she was fighting a losing battle. She finally agreed to follow him up the spiral staircase, in order to end the argument, in order to stop his agitation as well; she'd pushed open the baroque armoire's heavy doors and she'd started climbing the stairs with unimaginable difficulty—more than once she'd almost missed a step and nearly fell, because of the dark, she said. He was already far ahead, she could hear his steps on the stairs, but her own legs weren't responding, her limbs were heavy and stiff, she was having to make a concerted effort to put one foot in front of the other. She could feel a cool breeze on her face. Her steps were making a sharp cracking sound, the sound of tiny dead branches being broken (was she crushing a microscopic forest beneath her soles), it was impossible to make out the shapes around her, she was trying to imagine the surface she was stepping on, just dirty steps, covered with a thick film of dust or trash dropped over the years—she'd tried to count the stairs to slow her heartbeat, but that strange sound was growing louder with every step. Even the least slip or fall on the spiral staircase, she'd said, would spell certain death; she knew that of course, and at that moment she was convinced he was trying to kill her, or at least cause her accidental death. Climbing the spiral stairs was a real ordeal for her since she'd always suffered from vertigo, an ordeal that could have easily ended in tragedy; she'd been forced to stop on the stairs, she'd called for my father but he hadn't answered, he'd already forgotten about her, he must have closed the door behind him after he'd entered the room. She ended up going back down on her hands and knees, she'd felt strange things under her hands as she went, the touch of a dry substance mixed with dust, not simply dust, but something desiccated and crumbly that was bothering her skin, perhaps causing a slight irritation—she'd immediately thought she would catch a skin disease, a rash, and she said to herself: I'm calling a doctor as soon as possible. She'd caught her breath at the bottom, unable to figure out how much time had elapsed, she'd gone up to a window to examine her hands, and seeing a crushed fly's corpse in the crevice of her palm, she'd finally understood the cause of the uncomfortable sensation; she'd remained there staring at the mummified insect, its severed legs embedded in her palm, as though reading her future there in her open hand, the insect's tiny dismembered body forming a lone word, but no matter how hard she tried, turning her hand toward the daylight, she was unable to decipher it.

75. One thing was for sure, from the moment he'd set up his headquarters on top of the tower, in a tiny room filled with books and brochures and all the materials necessary for the work of thought, he'd stopped frantically measuring the villa, as though he'd given up for good the idea of making drawings based on actual measurements. Were we really supposed to believe that the air was somehow purer at the top of the tower, or that his lungs had found there something like a favorable amount of humidity, an atmosphere particularly suited to the work of the mind?

76. In the tower reigns a silence suited to thought, he said, up there he can escape the sound of the waves and pursue his reflections under the best circumstances. He had finally found the ideal atmosphere, he said several times, he told

himself he would finish his work right there, and that he wouldn't leave the tower—where this ideal atmosphere reigns—until he'd put the final touches on his plans for the renovation. For some elaborate reason, which he is at a loss to explain, he has decided to stay holed up on top of the corner tower—to be honest, he spends most of his time up there, cut off from the rest of the villa and the world at large. At first it was merely well suited to his thinking, to his attempts to clarify matters, but now the tower's atmosphere has—after several weeks of intense intellectual activity—become necessary, even indispensable to his endeavor to think through and explain, to his ceaseless work that sooner or later would allow him to discover the mathematics of the ideal villa, as he was fond of saying. If it wasn't for this room at the top of the tower, he'd never have been able to move forward with his work, never have been able to develop all those useful ideas that were necessary for him to proceed with his plans—that's why he'll likely never leave the tower, which has become for him the site of his ideal life.

77. Was his thought-work just an excuse to isolate himself? Still, there's no denying he'd seemed increasingly strange since moving into the corner tower, irascible and unpredictable, as though he'd become a caricature of himself, my mother had said.

78. And though it was seemingly built of the same materials, and according to the same principals of engineering that had guided the construction of the villa, the corner

tower had always struck him as being separate in some way from the rest of the building—that it was built on the edge of a rock overlooking the sea was probably not unrelated to this impression. They couldn't avoid it, nor figure out exactly how the tower was meant to fit in with the rest of the façade. But this sense of strangeness had only grown from the moment my father had—so to speak—set up his headquarters there, spending most of his time in this room at the top of the tower, where everything was askew, the objects and furniture having apparently come to a precarious arrangement. So his trips to the corner tower had become more frequent and lasted longer, the day he installed a cot recovered from one of the bedrooms on the third floor, my mother understood that he'd turned a corner and that there was nothing she could do to change his mind. From that day forward, he'd stopped wandering the villa, restricting his trips to a minimum; he'd become sparing with his own movements, measuring his words and breath as if henceforth his new life would obey a strict accounting. When she would enter that cramped room, she would feel threatened, besieged by the idea that she might disappear at any moment. She couldn't help but think that he'd taken up residence there not to think but simply in order to get away from his own thoughts, he was cut off not only from the outside world there but from himself as well, the renovation project probably now amounted to little more than an empty murmur in his brain. He was following a completely different design, she couldn't help but think, while still fearing that he might secretly have decided to get rid of her in order to achieve his ends. She thought she probably meant nothing more to him than a deformed reflection of an unjustifiable presence, each day receding more into the background, her presence rendered in part necessary by the habitual nature of her visits. And indeed every time she would get close to him and lean toward him, she would feel like he was staring—perplexed—at her soul, not just her image; my mother saw herself in my father's eyes as a stranger.

79. He'd carried upstairs and stored in the tower a jumble of objects and furniture recovered from various other rooms in the villa; he'd so easily taken possession of these things, which from now on would form an integral part of his universe, creating around him an unreal, suffocating atmosphere. What kind of man had he become? What was he doing, stuck for hours, and soon for days, surrounded by that stultifying decor? The clock on the wall behind him didn't tell the time. The project to renovate the villa was apparently little more than a vague memory, and even that was about to vanish, escape. The cot, the camping stove, the small worktable, but all sorts of useless things as well, brass doorknobs, a three-masted ship in a bottle resting on a console, a cane, several shells as well as the murmur they contained, stacks of booklets tied with a string—she used to look at all this as though through a shop window. Even the cans and jelly jars on the shelves had looked like museum pieces, she'd noted.

80. When you enter the room, it takes a minute to get used to the strange ambient light, but once your eyes adjust, it seems everything is slowly, inexorably converging toward the center. The shelves buckling under the weight of books and cans, the lamp with its olive shade, boxes filled with sketchbooks, the camping stove, the framed black and white photo of the villa: All the furniture is moving, millimeter by millimeter, toward the midpoint of the room, right where my father has put his worktable. He has always insisted that nothing be touched inside this room devoted to reflection, and that nothing be added either, unless it was some waste product of his work or part of the cascade of dust endlessly falling, which was quickly becoming— so to speak—what he cherished most in this world.

81. She was still reluctant to enter, holding her breath on the threshold. Please turn out the light, he would ask in a distant, almost mechanical voice, a voice in which you could feel the pain of his exclusion. That voice, she was thinking, could belong to an animal. The sound of her footsteps on the stairs must have been a nagging tendril digging into the margins of his thoughts, and now that she was only a few feet from him, standing motionless behind the half-open door, he surely took the sound of her breathing as the herald of an approaching threat, whose nature was as yet uncertain, concealed in a corner of her brain. For an instant, she imagined how he would criticize her once he found her there, and the idea that he might get angry or simply sulk at her in his typical black mood made her consider just turning around. He gave her that same vacant, skeptical look, the one he'd greet her with every evening; in that look she'd many times read his wariness when it came to anything that might suggest how pointless their efforts had been since moving into the villa. You're pale, she stammered, as she noticed the elongated shape of his bony feet sticking over the edge of the small bed. He asked her: What time is it? She ignored his question, it was all she could do to reconstruct it mentally, as though she were check-

ing its structure, experiencing its solidity in the rarified air of the
room. Daylight was fading outside the window. She turned off
the lone bulb hanging from the ceiling and she turned on a small
shaded lamp, which was sitting on a chair. She felt further dis-
couraged by the sight of this cheap lamp recovered from somewhere in the villa, but even more so by the dozens of snapshots
strewn across the floor, under the cot, stuck between the pages of
books. Arranged in this dim light, the objects and furniture appeared strange and hostile to her. Again she looked at his face: His
migraines made him unrecognizable, inaccessible. His exhaustion
was being transmitted to the furniture, which was slumped in
dark recesses of the room, furniture whose own breathing she
was sure she could hear. Now she wanted to get closer to him, to
touch him (perhaps to make sure that he was real and that they
were both in the same room); she wanted to prod him to get
up, but she saw his closed lids, his lashes, the unshaven patches
around his cheeks, and she noted that these overly detailed visions nauseated her. She thought for an instant that my father
was perhaps made out of a substance different from that of other
men, and that if she were to brush up against him, she might disappear. Still, she couldn't get mad at him. He was ashamed, angry
at himself for appearing that way, she thought right away, and as
she moved in the half-light, she had the impression the objects
were receding within the cramped space, worrying then that she
too would end up swept away by their movement. He'd pressed
his back against the headboard, trying in vain to get up. It wasn't
the first time she'd found him like this. He'd been forced again to
stop in the middle of the afternoon because of his headaches, and
it suddenly struck her, whenever she came to see him, not without a certain dread, that he might simply explode; she was always
pretending she could help him piece together the plans that the

migraines had scattered. When he got like this, did he still believe it was possible to improve their situation, even in the slightest? She was seeing things for what they were, she imagined his brain saturated with noise, itself become an overbearing nuisance. His migraines would sometimes bother him for days, not allowing his tired body to sleep, to the point where his personality seemed irrevocably changed. You can't stay like this. She heard her own voice, perfectly calm yet exterior to her own person. She knew he would refuse to see a doctor, no matter how hard she tried to tell him that he needed to rest, to get his mind off of things. And maybe I'm talking to a mirage, maybe we're in a dream, she said to herself. All the same, she made him get up and wash his face with cold water. Just like every evening, all he said was: I'll be down later.

82. And little by little, his almost insignificant quirks, which took the form of forgetfulness, losing things, and occasional outbursts of anger, were rearranged into symptoms of a profound derangement.

83. Once he'd decided to set up shop there, he never wanted to leave the room, as though he feared someone might gain access in his absence. Was he afraid she might disturb his notes, was he hiding something from her? His schedule, his habits, his infrequent movements, the way he could make her understand him without moving his lips: she guessed that from now on his movements would be economical and painstakingly

planned. He stuck to a careful set of coordinates, which probably allowed him to maintain a semblance of control in the face of a deeper disorder. Yet she'd done nothing to dissuade him from altering his life in this way, speaking and acting in his presence as though nothing had changed; since she too was convinced the villa would close in on them like a trap if she showed the slightest sign of weakness.

84. And indeed he felt like he was leading an entirely abstract existence, one that was separate from her own, for he was lost in a world of thoughts, of sounds and sensations that bore no relation to her world, and which weren't even distant allusions to the thoughts she was having, to the sounds and sensations she was experiencing, and in those moments when she would join him in the tiny corner bedroom, which almost hung on the edge of the world outside the villa itself, it was as though she was there to make certain he was still alive, to make sure she could recognize his voice when he criticized her or complained, but neither the brightness of his wide-open gray eyes nor the features of his face could convince her that she was with him. At moments like this she wouldn't know if she was his wife or rather a nurse keeping up a strained relationship with a stranger, hopelessly trying to maintain a banal and rambling conversation whose structure was threatening to collapse with each new sentence, but at the same time she was sure they were fighting a common enemy, thinking I'm not going to stop fighting, I'm not going to give up on him, convinced that they were both confronting the same existential difficulty—she was finding it comforting to behave with him as she would a sick child.

85. That's why, once it was clear he wasn't coming out of his den, she'd opted for raising indoor plants. Besides, she'd found on the premises—in the basement of the villa—all the tools necessary for their cultivation. Her trip to the basement, flashlight in hand, hadn't been in vain; far from it, since she'd discovered dozens of flowerpots among the jumble of prehistoric, broken-down things, and a collection of seed packets, sealed away in hermetic metal boxes, in glass jars marked with labels now eaten away. Exploring basements was never disappointing, she said, it could even be highly instructive—as proof she'd even uncovered several treatises on botany, as well as diverse scientific works dealing with the vegetable world. It was always amazing what you could store in basements and cellars, objects that would dwell for years tucked away down there—that's what she'd always thought. You'd sometimes find entire libraries, hundreds, sometimes thousands of books stored under a house in conditions disastrous for their preservation. The high levels of humidity typically found there causes books to decay, sometimes faster, sometimes slower, but always without fail. She'd grabbed the botany book and continued to search around, convinced that there were other treasures to be found in the cellar. Basements, she'd said, can conceal all kinds of things, for the most part broken and useless, but sometimes you find things that are perfectly fine, objects that could wind up being incredibly valuable to the person who finds them. One day these objects ceased to be useful and, as a result, they became something that's only in the way, which is why it was decided to put them in cellars and basements. It's impossible to imagine a house without a basement, just as it's absurd to want to dig a cellar without a house. All these objects that have lost their usefulness sink into oblivion in cellars, their common fate is to be forgotten, forgotten in cellars that form a parallel universe under apartment buildings and houses, whose existence most people never suspect. These objects are liable to remain forgotten for years, and then suddenly they'll be rescued from oblivion by some circumstance, an unexpected event that allows them years later to regain their function and escape being forgotten. The objects warehoused in the villa's basement were of no use to anyone, yet, nonetheless, someone had kept and stored them under the villa, on basement shelves, in damp boxes.

86. She'd fetched the pots, arranging dozens of them, of various shapes and sizes, around the outside of the villa—artistically—so that the rain could rinse them off; and while she was waiting for the rain to do its job, she'd deciphered the names of plants, the warnings on packets, and without delay she'd immersed herself in the treatise on botany. She'd turned the damp pages of the book she'd brought up from the basement, taking advantage of the moment to develop and perfect her understanding of nature, and more precisely of plants, assimilating the name and characteristics of each species of plant—and so, thanks to the botany treatise, she was able to accumulate all the knowledge necessary to realize her gardening project. A few days later, she'd arranged the flowerpots and window boxes at various strategic places inside the villa, places she'd determined in advance by taking into consideration the ideal lighting conditions for each species. She'd placed different-sized flowerpots on the windowsills and in the bay windows, still going about things like an artist, not simply according to scientific principals, as she made sure to point out. Thus she'd taken advantage of the numerous windows and other light sources in the villa in order to cover each floor with dozens of flowerpots, in this way she'd created an indoor greenhouse, transforming the entire villa into a botanical garden in a matter of weeks. She would wander the villa each day, armed with gardening implements and botanical precepts, going into rooms to check her flowers' growth—and the villa's corridors had become garden paths that reached across many floors. She'd watched over her crop with the severity of a boarding-school mistress, looking after each potted plant as though it were a tiny being—threatened in some way—that she was supposed to protect with all her skill. Several times a day, she would lean over a particular plant as though at the bedside of a sick child demanding her care and constant attention. She was totally devoted, attentive to each plant's growth, as if her own existence depended on it.

87. For weeks, this activity had effectively taken up all of her time; she hadn't thought of anything else for weeks, and she was finally able to ignore and forget all the unpleasantness of her new existence. As long as she was devoting herself to the task of planting and gardening, she was able to turn a blind eye to the villa's faults, and more or less acclimate to living there—she'd been granted a respite, at last she'd been able to reside comfortably in the villa, without being tortured by the ugliness of the worn wallpaper or the sight of cracks in the ceiling. And as it turns out, after a few weeks the results were greater than she could have hoped for, her plants had grown remarkably. It seems the villa had encouraged the plants to grow, to the point where it was almost inconceivable—the villa had become a giant greenhouse. The plants, she'd said, were showing that she was capable of incredible things. Certain plants had reached extraordinary and unexpected dimensions, greedily absorbing the window's light; she was transfixed by these plants at first, their hues taking on variable intensities depending on the time of day, they would exude these dreamlike images, she'd said, visions she couldn't quite describe. She'd felt a certain pride at being the author of these dream visions, and in the beginning at least the growth of the plants had reawakened her aesthetic impulse. But the success of her crops soon turned sour. She'd become dizzy on several occasions and she was tempted to attribute these spells to the different subtle scents emanating from the various plants. She'd developed a hypersensitivity to smells, and she'd begun to fear that each plant's fragrance was delivering a coded message, the toxicity of which was growing by the day, or perhaps hour. It wasn't long before the sight of the lush indoor plants had become a negative influence; she'd felt oppressed, and she'd been frightened to see just how far this invasion would go, to the point where she was beginning to think someone was playing a trick on her by adding even more plants while she wasn't looking. The vegetation was always in her thoughts, she used to wake up in the middle of the night thinking she could hear foliage rusting in the villa, she would listen carefully in the dark and she would think she could hear leaves knocking against the windows and doors. The leaves were forever shuddering, she'd thought, as though expressing some kind of terrible exaltation. And she'd imagined a heart was beating inside every plant, a tiny obstinate heart, always demanding more oxygen, more light. During the day, her eyes were in the habit of looking for this rustling, and every time she would enter a room an unfathomable fear gripped her—she was convinced the plants would start shaking the moment she came in, and to her the leaves were so many tongues—hundreds or even thousands of little sardonic tongues, looking to lick her body. She decided to give up gardening, overnight; she poured bleach in the pots, feeling strangely happy to administer the poison, she wasn't even brave enough to dispose of the dead flowers, she couldn't bear to hear another word about plants.

88. As a matter of fact, I wasn't even sure who was worse off, my mother or my father. Even in her first letter, she'd sounded depressed to me, like a depressive, hunted by something malicious. And you know I wasn't even that surprised, since I'd always known deep down that my mother was somewhat prone to melancholy. A depression that had taken its time before making its move, or so I was telling myself, employing various ruses and diversions so as to go unnoticed, growing quietly in the dark, until one day you have no choice but to see yourself in it.

89. She was sitting in the armchair, the one covered in threadbare mustard velvet, while all around her pots containing wilted flowers were forming a magic circle. She was aware just how ugly and uncomfortable this chair was, without quite being able to get up. She would have liked to not touch the chair, her elbows tight against her body, her spine a few centimeters from the back, knees held together and ankles crossed beneath her, so as to touch the floor with only the toe of a slipper, completely focused on her efforts to take up as little space as possible. She would have liked to close her eyes and wake up somewhere else, as though it were all a bad dream—then she would just have to get up and take a shower, and with clean, fresh-smelling clothes against her skin, she would be ready right away to resume a normal life. But she was still muttering to herself that they'd stolen it all, that all this furniture, that the villa's contents would never belong to them. She was worried her belongings were getting mixed up with these things that had belonged to strangers, strangers who were perhaps now dead—one day her own effects might end up the same way. She was afraid her things were becoming infected, contaminated through contact with this worn-out stuff. She dreamed of leaving for a safe place, someplace pristine where she could wash her hands, take a shower, put on fresh clothes.

90. When she found the keys just hanging there, on a nail in the closet under the stairs, she'd immediately thought of the abandoned bedroom on the second floor—this thought had crossed the dark closet like a spark. Since finding the bedroom door locked that first day, they hadn't tried to open it, they had never mentioned the room again and never once had they tried to get inside; they'd acted as though the room didn't exist and they'd actually managed to forget about it. How could it be that she'd only noticed the keys now, each week she would stack cartons of water under the stairs; despite his reassurances, she'd never been able to drink the tap water—no, she wouldn't have drunk that water for anything in the world, water she still thought infected, a carrier of germs and disease. Without thinking, she'd grabbed the keys and climbed straight to the second floor; she'd acted on a sudden impulse, as though she already knew what she would find there—at least she wasn't afraid, or

anxious; gripping the keys in her hand she'd slipped on a step, and as in a dream she'd suddenly found herself in front of the door, she'd grabbed a key at random, there were all kinds of different keys, flat keys, old-fashioned round keys, covered in rust, but she'd found it on the first try, and with the key now in the lock, it was all she could do to stifle a scream, meanwhile the door had opened almost by itself, and as in a dream she'd entered; the first thing she'd noticed was the hospital smell, a neon bulb was emitting a uniform light, this light had switched on just as she had turned the doorknob, she thought. She'd proceeded cautiously, looking around at walls the color of gray sand. There was nothing to discover here: no clue, no crack. The smooth walls made it seem as though the room had just been repainted. And perhaps because of the impeccable cleanliness, the uncharacteristic odor, she'd felt far away from everything, sealed inside a watertight world, with thick bulkheads, having forgotten the secret code to the metal door she'd unlocked on the way in.

91. Then, looking down at the floor (she didn't know how long she'd been there), she discovered a row of jars, dozens, perhaps hundreds of transparent jars, all the same size and diameter, each containing a reddish liquid, the color of bricks. The level of the liquid varied imperceptibly in each jar, so that the whole formed a diminishing wave: a kind of indoor oceanic garden, she thought, a sterile wave, biopsied and captured (as though for observation in a lab), cleverly divided among the receptacles arranged on the polished floor. A disturbing arrangement at that: The preserved wave, motionless, arrested in its movement, seemed to span two moments in time separated by an abyss. And this liquid, probably a pharmaceutical solution, but who knows, it could also be unstable and corrosive, perhaps even explosive if you shook it or it came in contact with air. The reality of what she saw didn't seem to want to register in her, she was having to concentrate to preserve it, so that the sight would be etched in her. And because she was having difficulty assembling this image, her experience of it lacked a unified tonality, as though separated by a pane of emotions, desires, deep inside her: as though she were seeing the wave in some forgotten distance.

92. In her moments of exhaustion or boredom, she would find it a relief to think about the laboratory bedroom. She'd imagine the rigid discipline, the bittersweet control found in careful, precise gestures, those belonging to the person who had arranged the jars, poured the brick-red liquid, being careful not to spill a drop, noting an infinitesimal difference in the level from one jar to the next, pouring out the excess liquid when necessary, measuring a new amount, perhaps redoing the operation several times over, until the perfect amount was reached. She would always see the scene in black and white, and the images would appear to jump, as in a silent film, disturbing the calm order of the gestures, producing an uneven cadence, like that of a heart. Wiping each jar first with a coarse cloth to eliminate all traces of dust and fingerprints (but surely he was wearing rubber gloves), then pouring the sterile preparation, taking stringent precautions, using measuring vials of various sizes, bending down to the floor to check the level, almost kneeling as though in prayer, and placing the jar in its precise place, determined to the nearest millimeter, repeating the identical operation without once departing from his self-possessed manner. He'd likely proceeded just as calmly when sculpting this lone wave, as though he were performing a ritual, a scalpel's precision delineating each movement within a monotonous succession, held taut by secret threads.

93. But when his headaches would leave him alone for a few hours, or sometimes even several days, his face would take on a strange air of satisfaction, approaching meanness. She would look at him and see the contrast between the middle and upper regions of his face—the verticality of his aquiline nose between predatory gray eyes, too close together; his shifty, greedy, almost fanatical gaze in opposition to the depressive, shy insolence of his forehead, suggesting either cowardice or extreme concentration. She sensed he was through with drawing up plans for the villa, and that from now on his only purpose in life would be to further the abandonment and even the ruin of their plans to start anew. And whenever he spoke to her his words would always take the form of a cautionary tale, and then she would see that he was done trying to convince her, or pique her interest; as far as he's concerned, my acquiescence or refusal is beside the point, my mother had written, it's almost like he doesn't even think I'm able or have the right to understand, to agree or disagree with him, because this right, or more to the point this faculty, has for a reason known only to him been henceforth rescinded. And when she stood in front of my father, my mother continued to look for that last particle of impressionable being, something she could touch and restore to good sense.

94. In the end, they were no longer communicating, except by means of brief notes left on the corner of a table. Who knows, maybe my mother was collecting these enigmatic messages in a shoebox, in hopes of one day finding some way to decode them.

95. And when he would agree to come down to the living room, seemingly in a conciliatory mood, as though ready to start up a real conversation with her, or, who knows, perhaps he would suggest they take a little drive or go for a walk along the cliffs, she was always performing some familiar task (wiping an object, opening a desk drawer) as though she wanted to present him with a simulacrum of normal life, and then she would feel as though she were waking from a bad dream and that now they could start again from scratch, forgetting about their disappointments, straightening out their affairs, finding a place for everything inside a house that would be familiar, arranged to their taste.

96. The villa was her only world, she'd said, and indeed as soon as she would have to leave, taking the car to the nearest shopping center, she would feel she was floating through a contrived world, whose laws she'd forgotten; she would feel even more lost, in fact, as though she wasn't meant to live in that world. She would push a cart down the aisles of the store, automatically grabbing products as though she were connected to another world via secret threads, ready to break at the slightest misstep.

Christmas was approaching and everything was awash in holiday preparations: decorations and strands of electric lights, aisles overflowing with toys, stuffed animals, video-game consoles. Noticing her slow meanderings, salespeople would sometimes approach her to draw her attention to some promotion or other. She would avoid looking at them, for fear of being discovered.

97. Then she would find herself in the vast parking lot, darkened by the waning light. The headlights of the cars would blind her as they left the shopping center. There would be nothing in front of her but a long disgusting asphalt beach, cut into squares; the garish colors of the supermarket's neon sign standing out against the blood-red sky. She would arrive home only after having driven for hours on country roads, their gentle curves getting lost in the evening twilight. And when she would turn off the ignition, the sound of the motor would continue to resonate inside her head.

98. Back home in the villa, she'd perpetually wait for something to happen—and whether it did or didn't happen, she was afraid all the same. She had no idea what this thing could be. Then the rows of jars would come to mind and she found herself wishing they would indeed explode, spreading their corrosive liquid across the floor, starting a fire.

99. Now and then, when she was feeling especially bored or listless, she would open a moving box at random, as if to make sure their things were still there. Was she afraid they'd evaporated during the move? That's how she found my old school notebooks, notebooks she'd kept and then forgot, notebooks turned black by the weather and heavy as lead. She'd packed these boxes years ago, like all parents do once their child has become an adult and left home. She wouldn't have been able to tear those notebooks up for anything in the world, nor even been able to part with them—that's why she'd filed them away in boxes. We pack these boxes without having the slightest idea what we'll do with them, in all likelihood such boxes are completely useless and we know it, even as we're packing them, not that this stops us from completing our task. It's enough to know that boxes like this exist and that they are stored somewhere, when possible in a dry place. We don't know why we attach so much importance to the boxes or why we want to keep them at all cost—frankly, these boxes remain hermetically sealed more often than not, and their contents never again see the light of day, for the simple reason that no one thinks to open them.

100. Your entire childhood is here, my mother had written, you could show up at any moment, you might decide to come and pay us a visit in the villa, just to make sure your childhood has remained intact, and you would find your toys, your clothes, you would find your old notebooks filled with your childhood writings. The bedroom you had as a child doesn't exist anymore, but your entire childhood is here, contained in these boxes, it's true, my mother had written. Your toys and your

school notebooks haven't been destroyed, she said; they've been preserved in their original state, and are somewhere in the ballroom, with all our stuff, in boxes. We could unpack the boxes containing your childhood toys and things, and we could arrange all these possessions in a bedroom converted to that purpose—we could create a bedroom in the villa, specially conceived to house all your childhood things, and if you wanted you could go through all these toys and notebooks from your childhood, you could reread Krafft-Ebing, you could even fill up new notebooks if you liked, in that way perfectly recreating your childhood bedroom. You know the tiny grand piano we gave you when you turned three, and that you broke that same day, not accidentally but on purpose—the one we got fixed and that you broke a second time, with the same fury? It was an exact replica of a concert piano, and from it we never heard a single chord, let alone a melody, just a cacophony of infernal, frightening notes, notes that reflected your own senseless will to destroy—well, that tiny copy of a piano is still here, carefully wrapped in a gray cover. We'll eventually find a place for it in the villa. You never touched that piano, save to extract discordant sounds from it; from your earliest days, you disliked everything musical, you rebelled against the very music you were playing, and against the music you were listening to, you showed your musical hatred by plugging your ears every time I started to play piano or put on piano music—it took years for you to get over this hatred and agree to listen to piano music. It didn't matter that we wanted to instill in you a rudimentary knowledge of music, we shouldn't have tried to force musical training on you, for your entire being has always been in revolt against music and the music world. We should also never have given you that violin a couple of years later, the one you broke right in front of us by smashing it against the wall. It was crazy to think the violin would bring you back to music, or rather, I should say (my mother had written) bring you back to musical training. You steadfastly refused to play a musical instrument, you refused to have anything to do with them, as though you were furious at them. You had no desire to have a relationship with a musical instrument, and in fact you were completely incapable of having such a relationship. With all your body and soul, you rejected music and musical instruments, and with all your might you stood in the way of your musical training. There was no use insisting, there was no way to teach you music. Playing the piano would have ended up killing you, I realized much later; I often used to think as well, what a mistake it was wanting you to learn piano. Music can't be taught by force, music can't be taught to someone who refuses to give himself to music, someone who resists, with all his might, the musical impulse. Our determination to teach you music almost extinguished every last ounce of innate musicality you might have possessed, a little bit more and you'd have been furious at music forever. My attempts to teach you music were always fruitless and counterproductive—attempts that could only ever have led to utter failure, your father said. That's why not just the tiny piano, but the training violin as well, had always been pointless and condemned to silence.

101. You used to get so much pleasure from covering the pages of your notebooks with your writing, my mother had said; no one ever asked you to fill up those notebooks, which you would demand, kicking and screaming, scribbling away as soon as you got them. You used to lock yourself in your bedroom, carrying the notebooks under your arm, you would be quiet for hours and we wouldn't hear a peep from your room, we knew you were studiously filling your notebooks, not quite sure if we should be thankful or not for having such a calm and quiet child. You'd decline to do anything else, and you'd refuse to play or leave your room, the sole objective being to continue writing without interruption. And as soon as you were finished marking up one notebook, you would demand another and immediately set to work, you would write more, and always without ever tiring. You used to spend hours cooped up in your room, you seemed to not need to run around like other children, you liked neither running nor playing with children your own age, you never showed any aptitude for sports—I used to often think you would never play sports, and that you would always be against physical activity. You used to copy down any and everything, my mother had said, in one notebook you'd copied out the "Second Preface" to *The Critique of Pure Reason*, while in another notebook it was the first forty pages of *Psychopathia Sexualis*, transcribed in its entirety without omitting a single comma. What could possibly have gotten into you to make you copy out the works of Krafft-Ebing, I still have no idea; I tried to imagine what a child your age could possibly get from Krafft-Ebing—until then, I had no idea such a book existed, and I wonder if your father even knew that this book was in the house. Until then, I knew nothing about Krafft-Ebing and his interpretation of sexual perversions, I hadn't even heard the name Krafft-Ebing, but I was able to read the first forty pages of his book—can you imagine, reading Krafft-Ebing in your childish handwriting, take my word for it, no mother is prepared for that.

102. Years later, my mother was standing in the vast ballroom, she'd opened a notebook at random, she'd seen me, and she'd recognized me right away. She was not so much looking at the words but seeing me, the child who had written the words, more or less straight onto the page, the child with the notebooks had suddenly resurfaced. You were once again there, she'd said, I'd shown up again, miraculously, or rather the way a jack-in-the-box pops out suddenly, I was standing there and my mother was unable to refute my childlike presence, this childhood wasn't simply a memory, nor was it entirely a dream, it was present before her eyes, and my mother could actually look at the child, she was looking at her introverted and unreachable son, it was that same lonely, brusque child, the one she wanted to hold and ask forgiveness of, without exactly knowing for what, she wasn't even sure she could speak to her son, was he at least able to hear her, she'd even stupidly wondered if he had ears to hear her with over there where he was standing, she'd thought for a moment she was dreaming, but the notebooks were there, they were bearing witness with their childlike scribble, and so she couldn't stop staring at the taciturn child who was still saying nothing, seeming just as uninterested in her as he'd ever been, she was staring as though at a living and mute enigma, without so much as a reply.

103. One morning, she heard a noise. It was strangely distinct, like the first time, three months earlier. He'd said it was a rat or a stray cat, but she was certain he hadn't heard a thing, and that she was the only one who had heard the noise. He'd offered this explanation (a rat or a stray cat) probably in order to reassure her, but he'd only managed to make her worry. They were no longer able to experience the same things, they were each locked inside different worlds—this was now obvious to her. He was locked in the tower world while she was locked in the ballroom world, it was futile and pointless to try to communicate anything, there was no bridge, those two worlds were not related. He was spending most of his time in the tower, and he'd adopted a way of thinking that was both characteristic of and inseparable from it, she was convinced. We live in different and incompatible worlds, even when we're in the same room we're apart, standing light-years from one another, as far away as possible. Everything he was capable of thinking—just like every word he was capable of speaking—had to be put in relation to the tower's atmosphere. He'd developed his own way of thinking in the tower, while she'd developed her own way of thinking in the ballroom, and there was no use trying to relate one mode of thought to the other. It couldn't be an animal noise, she'd thought, but she couldn't say anything more about the nature or source of this noise.

104. She felt like it was a planned intrusion, like the noise was conveying some kind of intension, it couldn't be an animal noise, she said. This had something intimate about it, like something is there, breathing the same air as you, a presence getting between you and the walls, floating in space. The noise gave you this impression, the impression that a body was there, disrupting space—she hadn't said this to my father, she'd only thought it.

105. It was the umpteenth letter she'd written to me, I never wrote back, calmly and consistently rebuffing her numerous attempts to get in touch with me; I wouldn't even so much as deign to open them, being content to nonchalantly glance at the handwriting on the envelope, throwing the letter just as nonchalantly in the basket as I would a leaflet or misleading ad once I'd recognized her writing, thinking: She's fucking obsessed with sending me these letters—or else: Is she ever going to give me a moment's peace—and a minute later, having forgotten about the crumpled paper at the bottom of the basket, I'd be trying as hard as I could to push her image further still into the folds of my brain. She had to be thinking the following: that I was beyond hope, that as far as I was concerned only one thing mattered (she was sure of this), that I finish my dissertation on Foucault, a dissertation begun years ago (it's true), and which I was still unable to finish (indeed), an obsession that had snuffed out any curiosity, any interest lying outside the realm of my philosophical preoccupations, an idée fixe that had wound up killing any sympathy I might've had for the world, and which in the end had cut me off from the world, making me indifferent to everything actually, including and above all else myself, making me incapable as it were of being interested in anything other than Foucault—yes, I've been living with Foucault mania for years (as she liked to put it) and, like a drug, I was under the influence of Michel Foucault. I'd read and reread Foucault's complete works, books that were no longer separate from me, were now a part of me; these works were a substance, solid and visible in the cramped space of my bedroom, and yet they'd somehow turned into mysterious, ungraspable entities whose contours and volume, whose surfaces, housed deep inside me, out of sight, made up an entire geography of confusion. I'd amass notes and scholarly remarks in the margins of these books, books that I could no longer distinguish from myself, I would fill folders with their recopied sentences, underlining Foucault's key phrases with a heavy, almost angry stroke; these were books I'd read and reread dozens of times, sentences I knew by heart, because they were inscribed in me down to my last cell, sentences I could've recited to you for hours. Michel Foucault: French philosopher, born in Poitiers 1926, died in Paris 1984. She'd read these words somewhere, that was the day she was to learn everything she would ever know about Foucault, a collection of boring facts and more or less scandalous anecdotes, and she would never try to find out more, forever associating the philosopher's name with motley masses of madmen, with perverts and the debauched, as well as with a suspect analysis of illness and human horrors; she'd felt a kind of detached curiosity as she read these few lines, which confirmed her suspicions, she was relieved finally as she read and reread, above all those two dates that seemed to suggest that the danger posed by his books had passed, that the corrupting powers of his mind had been neutralized. Perhaps she'd come across that strange photo of the philosopher in his bathrobe and wondered, seeing him there with his shaved head and ambiguous smile, what could have gotten into me to make me crazy about this intellectual in a dressing gown; 1926–1984 summed up like a tombstone everything she'd learned about him that day, thus allowing her to forget that photo—there was no longer any doubt, I'd fallen under the sway of a tyrannical mentor, my harsh master, the guru who had seduced and ruined me, the gay philosopher who had dulled my intellect and will. Not only would I never finish my dissertation, I'd also burned, one by one, every bridge along the way, depriving myself of any future, recognition, or greatness. I'd become a loser, really, or even some kind of monster (that much she'd gotten right), I'd lost touch with all my friends, I wasn't dating anyone, I hardly ever answered the phone anymore, and I would probably end up a mere shadow of myself, having forgotten that I even had genitals, and that somewhere in my chest a heart was still beating, blood still flowing through my veins—those were her thoughts on the matter of me, as she anticipated my fall and fears. I'd already completed part of the assignment, I used to say to myself, I'd deserted the lecture halls, I'd insulted my professors, abandoning forever the university, its libraries and somber colloquia, organized in confidence in the bowels of shabby buildings lit by neon; I would be neither a university professor nor a lecturer, it's as simple as that, I'd say to myself, I'll never publish a single sentence on Foucault, I'll never write anything at all; oh, perhaps I'll begin a novel, which in turn I'll abandon as well, leaving it to rot in some desk drawer—in a few years, I'll be a disillusioned spectator at my own failure, I'll be able to watch the shipwreck of my life, washed up on the other shore. And all this thanks to the genius of Foucault, she was surely muttering to herself, all this because of a philosopher who had died of AIDS, and had infected me with the philosophy bug in turn, encouraging me to make a desert of all that surrounded me, that's what philosophy leads to, if you ask me philosophy is a mortal sickness—that's what she was surely thinking, a sickness that isolates and destroys, she'd never really figured out what was contained in the works of this philosopher of prisons, hospitals, and barracks, she couldn't know how vital Foucault's work had become for me, but she knew my Foucault mania was tearing up her letters in my hands, preventing me from answering the phone, that same disease of thought which had made me cold and impervious to the stuff of emotions and desires. Mothers will comment on their sons' lives till the end of their days, and no one can do a thing about it, they'll elaborate upon their endless commentary concerning their sons' activities, their supposed feelings, and they won't be able to help but think that this eternal fiction, woven by them out of whole cloth, is the truth of the matter regarding their sons' feelings, given that a mother's instinct is never wrong, they'll always think. Commentaries we can make neither heads nor tails of, without any relation to reality, commentaries ceaselessly repeating inside your head, and which are nothing more than so many demolition projects, if you ask me. But it hadn't deterred her to know that I would contradict any statement, especially one coming from a mother, and it certainly hadn't stopped her from writing to me, to see how I was coming along with my Foucault mania. This extreme form of loneliness, which she'd dubbed Foucault mania, wasn't much of a concern anymore, she never received replies to her letters, and still she kept writing to me, without expecting me to return the gesture, she would imagine me locked in my tiny student accommodations, I was well past the age to be a student, yet unlikely to ever move out of this room, I was acting out my own confinement, performing to perfection my Foucault mania, never once letting my attention stray from my starring role. She wasn't expecting me to write back, she wasn't writing to receive a response, she would write more than twenty letters without even being sure I was reading them, she'd talked about the indoor plants, and all those rooms that seemed to tense up as soon as you entered, as if they were angry at you, or else reacting to some age-old fear; she'd discussed the renovations and my father's migraines, she could have easily found a thousand more things to talk about if she'd wanted to. Had it not crossed her mind to get in touch with my best friend, asking that old buddy to snoop around under a false pretext, asking him to take notes on everything he observed, analyze my most meaningless gesture, the way I walk, committing to memory everything I say, as a lab technician would, nothing would escape the notice of this aforementioned friend, he would provide a quasi-scientific description of my behavior, how I spent my time, information regarding my opinions, my intentions, a complete inventory of my ideas dealing with the notion of family, that's what she was demanding, did I speak readily about my parents, he would record the frequency with which I used the words "mother," "father," "parents" in conversation, describing in detail the expression on my face, the tone of my voice when I mention my mother, etc. Was he still listening to music, or had he thrown out all his records? He must have accumulated mountains of notes in the time he's been working on that dissertation of his, the title of which she'd heard once, a crazy title she'd quickly tried to forget, because it sounded so arrogant and unhinged. She used to imagine impressive piles of notes on his desk, she would also see editions of Foucault's works in the tiny bedroom, the complete works of the philosopher of prisons, as well as commentaries upon these works, fat annotated books gnawing away at the cramped space of his small bedroom, a bedroom that must resemble a paper mill, a closet is what she would like to say (more so than a bedroom), that's what he lives in, an enclosed space dedicated to Foucault, a sealed space where the Foucault mania had been allowed to flourish freely for years, spreading its wings above his thin face, he'd never been a pudgy child, but boy, after these past few years on the Foucault diet, morning, noon, and night, skipping meals, never going out, drastically cutting back all of his contact with the outside world, he'd had to have lost weight, to the point of being unrecognizable, looking himself like one of those AIDS patients floating in their baggy clothes, now he must resemble one of those prematurely aged intellectuals, dried-up by sleepless nights and an unhealthy diet, taking too many pills as had always been his habit, would he sometimes at least take a break to play records, was he still listening to the *Goldberg Variations*, the Glenn Gould version, as before, perhaps he'd gotten rid of everything, his books, his clothes, his grandfather's watch, his electric razor, maybe he'd taken down or shattered the mirrors, he'd maybe even thrown his computer out the window, but he'd likely kept the disc of the *Goldberg Variations*, yes he'd gotten rid of everything except the *Goldberg Variations*, she was remembering that his first impulse upon arriving in Sables (when he used to take advantage of our absence to hang out in the small apartment in Sables and catch up on his studies) was always to put on the Bach disc, before even turning on the heat and opening the shutters, he'd one day confided this detail to her about his time spent in that one-bedroom apartment in Sables, she'd never really known what he was up to when he used to spend weeks at a time there, the only thing she was sure of was that he used to shut himself up for days on end, and that his first reflex upon arriving was to listen to Bach played by Glenn Gould, the *Goldberg Variations*, he'd never have stood for another version, Glenn Gould or nothing at all he used to say (indeed), Glenn Gould now and forever (I'll confirm). But maybe she was wrong. Perhaps he'd bought a large stock of darts and was spending his days aiming at the target, a map of France tacked to the wall at the other end of the bedroom, perhaps he'd become an all-round champion at darts, planting the darts precisely where he wanted them on the road map, after all wasn't that better than imagining him under the influence of Foucault.

106.
While she was busy writing this letter, she heard it again. This time, the noise seemed determined to penetrate the thick walls, to travel across the room until it reached her. She'd just sat down to write a letter that would of course go unanswered, and which she would soon forget after she'd sent it, she tried to forget each letter she sent, a forgetfulness that would protect her, immunize her against the disappointment and rancor, this was the only way she could continue writing me. It (the noise) seemed to emanate from someone who wanted to be seen, while still remaining in the shadows, someone hesitant to make himself known, yet quietly insistent. It was an intentional noise, directed at her, she thought, aimed at her, and no one else; it was trying to distract her, to get her away from her writing, insinuating itself into her consciousness. It was the early warning signs of a presence, complete with everything that was threatening, worrying, and even reassuring about that presence, and for some reason, which she was unable to explain, she also sensed something familiar in it. She'd stopped writing her letter in mid-sentence (as the noise had seemed to demand), she knew at once that she would have to find out what it was before she could get back to her writing, and yet—she thought furtively—she wasn't sure what she would do if she found something, she couldn't swear that she wouldn't be forced to tear up, in a few minutes or a few hours, those pages covered in her writing, because perhaps she wouldn't be able to pick up the thread again, perhaps in reading these words she'd written earlier, she wouldn't be able to ascribe them any meaning. It hadn't even crossed her mind to ask my father or to let him know, she'd somehow known she was the only one who could solve the noise problem; and then, really, the very prospect of going to see him upstairs was just too discouraging. He hadn't heard a thing, probably, and anyway

he would just say again: It's just a stray cat, or a rat, without re-membering that he'd said the same thing last time. He was more than capable of that, since arriving in the villa, repeating sen-tences without thinking, oblivious to everything, especially to her uneasiness. The best-case scenario was that he'd perhaps try to reassure her, offering to inspect the villa to prove that there was nothing to worry about, that the villa was completely vacant, and that they were safe—but she was convinced, and there was noth-ing he could do to sway her; he would never rid her of the idea they weren't alone in the villa. And even if he were to convince himself that he'd heard something too, even if he were to pretend to look with her, climbing the stairs, opening the bedroom doors, inspecting the corridors, this would only push the noise away. It was too difficult to explain why, but now she was sure she'd been listening for this noise for weeks, maybe even years, and that she alone could hear it. Had she given up the piano simply in order to be more receptive? This noise, she'd said, had put her on the path to something, and now that it'd returned, she couldn't avoid looking for whatever it was any longer, so as to get to the bottom of things. So she'd stood up and she'd gone upstairs, the thought that she could get lost, that no one would come to her aid, making her vaguely apprehensive all the while. She'd opened doors, discovering snapshots of the villa left on ledges or strewn on the floor, abandoned photos testifying to my parents' failure to live like normal people in the villa, like normal people living in a house where each object tells a story, and where there are stable, stationary places, places where they could have lived, and where things would have happened, things that would have formed a kind of context. She found nothing. Once back downstairs, she glanced indifferently at the letter, and had trouble recognizing her own writing. The sentences she'd written now seemed far away, almost misleading. She was again convinced that I wasn't bothering to open her letters, she'd always basically suspected that I was capable of acting unjustly, or at least in a manner unworthy of a son, but she'd never quite had the nerve to admit to herself that I'd always been cold, egotistical, and that my eyes and voice had always contained the potential for real viciousness; now she knew, however, that I was a being capable of outright malice, and she wondered (it was the first time she'd formulated it this way, and she wasn't quite sure if it was a question or a statement): Did I manage to not understand my son.

107. The night before, my father had come in the middle of the night to lay next to her, without taking his clothes off. She couldn't remember how long it'd been since the last time she'd seen him, she'd felt him smiling in the dark. He smelled bad. She ended up falling asleep. The next morning, he'd disappeared.

108. She'd found it, or rather him, the next day in a small bedroom on the third floor. The thing was quite small and frail, and at first she'd taken him for a child still groggy from waking up, or perhaps he was under the influence of some medication? The general shape of his body and his narrow skull suggested some kind of pathology. He was sitting on the edge of the bed in his underwear. From the very first instant, she found the sight of him inevitable, unavoidable. This is what she told herself, as though it were all perfectly obvious:

He'd been there for days and perhaps weeks, he'd waited patiently without showing any interest in what was going on outside his bedroom, and he'll be no more willing to leave now than before. She never managed to figure out his age; he was short, or gave an impression of shortness, and there was something insipid about his features, he had a smooth face upon which emotion hadn't left any visible marks. She stared at him, trying in vain to locate some sign, anything that would have allowed her to identify him, and then she'd asked him how long he'd been there. Her words dangled there in the room, just out of her reach, and she felt in much the same predicament. She inspected the room, trying to recall the last time she'd been in this part of the villa, searching for a clue (for example, clothing or crumbs) that would prove he'd been there for days—she doesn't know why she needed to know he'd been there for some time.

109.

There was something evasive about his manner, out of focus, he seemed about to disappear from one minute to the next. Nevertheless, they were in the same room, and the only way out was through the door, which she was blocking as though she were afraid he might try to escape. She was still standing in front of him, he was seated, or more to the point hunched over, perched like a bird on a limb. He'd lowered his face. Was he by chance trying to communicate to her his feelings of distress? She wasn't convinced. How long have you been here, she'd muttered. You've been keeping an eye on us, weren't you? You've been watching our every move, and you were waiting for the right moment to make yourself known. She was certain, however, that he wasn't listening, and that perhaps he couldn't even hear her, something in his head was keeping him in the background, far away from her, as though he were located very, very far away, thousands of light years away, and so she was thinking that this face was only an image, an image that had crossed layers of time, and she should keep in mind that this wasn't his real face. We didn't notice you, but you were there, she'd added, making sure to articulate clearly with a pause after each word, and you were listening to us, weren't you? He was watching her, and he somehow seemed older now, due simply to the fact that his head was now raised, there had been a slight movement of his chin, his eyes, which were the basis of this metamorphosis, aging him. He looked as though he was trying to solve a complicated riddle. That is, unless my speech constitutes some sort of problem for him, like an equation to be solved, she thought. Or maybe he was deaf, that's all, can you tell if someone is deaf just by looking. She couldn't stop looking at him, nor stop trying to find clues in his unreadable face. She was finding it difficult to recall his traits. Could he at least get up, stand on his own legs, she'd wondered. Was he able to move about normally? He seemed so weak, exhausted, like after a long trip. She told herself she mustn't frighten him, that he must be exhausted after his long confinement in the bedroom.

110. She didn't know what he was feeling, and she wasn't sure what it meant for him to be discovered in someone else's house. He had nothing to do with this place, that was for sure, he couldn't possibly stay here any longer, she was repeatedly saying these things without really managing to convince herself—but was he at least dimly aware that he was an intruder, a stowaway of sorts? He had nothing to do with this place, so far as she could tell, but what could he possibly have to do with anywhere else?—that's what you would inevitably wonder if you saw him, and then you would inevitably feel sorry for him. She was telling herself that he'd escaped from a mental hospital, that she'd better call the asylums and clinics in the area, to see if any patients were missing, she was looking in the phonebook, writing down the numbers, and these simple, precise acts were helping her to lend a semblance of order to a situation that could have easily become confused, and even have degenerated, if she hadn't reacted. Every day, dozens of madmen were slipping their guards' notice, escaping from psychiatric institutions and blending in with their surroundings. Sometimes they were never heard from again, did they ever take refuge in abandoned houses? People who were stark raving mad just going up in smoke, disappearing into thin air. She had this image of fugitives running in their pajamas through the forest, scratches on their faces, on the exposed parts of their bodies. And perhaps he'd indeed believed that the villa was one of those vacant houses where he could take refuge, seek asylum. And there was something more upsetting about this idea than she'd initially reckoned. She'd thought the word asylum for a second time now (pronouncing it in her head), and the proximity of the word asylum to the word villa had given her a jolt of panic. She remembered how, in the first months of their stay, she'd paid particular attention to all those words that were disappearing from their vocabulary—she never knew to what extent this forgetting was intentional: words they were burying in the deepest recesses of their minds, but why? And as she stood in front of that diminutive being, she thought that she'd too long held this secret word (asylum) inside her, and now that it had slipped out, it was exerting its corrosive power upon the walls and floors of the villa.

111. But then again, assuming the drugs were rendering him senseless, how long would he remain in this state of torpor, and what would happen when the sedatives wore off? Might he suddenly become dangerous? But the drugs haven't affected his ability to feel, she reasoned. The proof being that he tried to communicate with us by using those noises, which were his words, so to speak, but we, of course, couldn't understand. She thought of all those sounds that escape from us without managing to become words, wondering too if anyone had ever thought to codify all the verbal content hidden behind simple movements. But then again, he couldn't have been unaware of their presence, he had to have picked up on their comings and goings, their expeditions into the spaces of the villa, and if he'd sat there for so long without signaling to them, it's because he had a reason to do so. Unless of course he's deaf, she thought for the second time. But then why hadn't he seemed startled, or even slightly concerned, when she'd opened the bedroom door, as though he'd expected her to walk in, almost like he was already familiar with her? Neither apathy nor indifference, she'd thought, but rather a limited ability to make out what was happening to him, to see the shape of the events that nonetheless involved him intimately. For example, she was now in the same room with him, and still she wasn't sure he was aware of being there with her. He was still sitting on the bed, unreal, and she was standing in front of him, but he was no more concerned about her than he would have been in the presence of an object, a piece of furniture.

112.

All these new connections forming in our brains when we are faced with the unknown. We have to get used to unconsciously modifying an untold number of parameters, just to take in this new face, these unheard-of gestures, the sound of a new, perhaps unique voice, so as not to confuse a stranger with someone else. Our consciousness becomes trained—unwittingly—in a new way of seeing, of perceiving.

113.

Actually, she'd never seen a crazy person before. Was she going to have to adjust her vision, change her way of seeing, in order to see him properly, in order to see him and not someone else? What did she have to lose? He might bite her hand, start beating his head against the wall. She'd heard all kinds of stories about the sick and insane, locked up in padded rooms and heavily sedated. She felt no fear in his presence, however. She wasn't worried, she didn't feel threatened by him. She wasn't sensing any violence in him at all, she was convinced he wasn't capable of violence. And even if someone had told her he'd escaped from a cell in a psychiatric hospital, she wouldn't have been afraid, and she wouldn't have tried to get away from him. He seemed rather like a foundling (and apparently she was the one who had found him, at least that's what she was telling herself), and she was the only one who knew he'd been found there, a few minutes or a few hours ago, right there in the same room as her, and perhaps she alone knew he existed.

114. Talk to me if you want. I'm speaking but I can be quiet too. I can make myself as fragile as you, I can act as if I'm not really here. As she finished speaking these sentences, she was blinded for a moment by the realization that something wasn't right with their structure; she thought she could see a break or a slight crack in them, somehow, as though she were examining an X-ray of an injured limb in a light box. She heard herself say again: You don't know who I am either, without being sure that her words were reaching him—she saw her words as still floating in midair, her sentence drifting by like a sad cloud. And introducing herself, saying her own name, gave her a real start, almost made her turn and run, as if it hadn't happened to her in years, hearing her name spoken aloud. She was also perhaps aware of how pathetic her attempts were to lend a touch of normalcy to a situation that remained, despite everything, rather complicated, to put it mildly. But why, after all, should she care if the situation seemed natural, why should she try to strip it of all its ambiguity, why should she continue to act in his presence as though it were normal for him to be here?

115. She said to him (in a voice that seemed to her shallow and lacking in seriousness): I'm going to get some clothes, don't move, I'll be back in a minute. And right away, she'd felt relieved by this detached, almost forced tone. Hearing it, she felt that she was taking control of the situation, so to speak. She pushed the door shut when she left, as a precaution, without fully closing it, however, as if to show the occupant that he wasn't a prisoner, and then she carefully proceeded to the living room. And once she was alone again, she tried to continue their conversation in her head, consciously pushing aside the idea that, thus far, he hadn't said a word, and that strictly speaking they hadn't communicated at all. All that mattered in her eyes was that they'd met, and neither one had been afraid, nor had tried to run away. And since he'd seemed to her like a child (at least at certain moments), she more or less decided that she would be a sort of mother to him, full of concern, because he was, perhaps, an orphan—traumatized.

116. She could always take him straight to the hospital, in that case she would get him dressed and fill a bag with clothes that might fit him, and she would drop him off at the door, explaining that she'd found him walking on the side of the road, that he was unable to say where he was going. She wouldn't say a word about the villa, the strange noises, the bedroom in which she'd found him, almost naked; she didn't want to go into details, she knew that recounting the details would only make her look suspicious, and perhaps they would ask questions, questions that would only make her uncomfortable and drag her still further into the matter, so that in the end they would open an investigation, suspecting that she'd kidnapped the child and held him captive—who knows, maybe all of this would land her in jail. One thing was certain, she was thinking, he seems to have ended up where he wanted to, he wasn't there by chance. But, then again, she could only imagine his will as being like an ensemble of small, imperfect movements, whose combination somehow produced a concrete result, almost in spite of itself. Something completely devoid of intention, that is, thus incapable of duplicity. No, she wouldn't end up opting for any of those solutions.

117. Upon her return, he'd disappeared. She thought she'd entered the wrong bedroom by mistake, she inspected all the rooms on the floor to no avail. When she got back to the room, which she didn't recognize now that he was gone (but perhaps she just hadn't paid attention the first time), she went ahead and left the clothes on the bed.

118. Now that she was alone again, she went over everything that had happened since moving into the villa, and already another story was beginning to form in her head, a story with a tightly wound plot, full of uncertainty, where much is left unsaid, and in which she was playing the leading role. He'd managed to get into the villa, and he'd been happy there—but for how long had he really been there, and why had he chosen the villa and not some other house in the surrounding area? And even if he did break into the villa by chance, he must have felt a little at home, for he was still there, he'd stayed put, as though his presence was somehow necessary. She was trying to understand, in hopes this would lend a precise meaning to the fact that he was there in the villa and not somewhere else, she was trying to assign a seemingly mundane explanation to his enigmatic presence. And her sense that he too had no idea what he was doing there only complicated matters further; or, if he did know, it was only within the bounds of his diminished capacity. She was trying to recall what she'd been doing these past few days, what she'd been feeling, thinking, but the effort seemed enormous, out of proportion to the task, insane. Everything was happening as if to someone else, and she was now beginning to realize that her memory was filled with false information. She felt almost as though she were digging a hole whose walls were collapsing with each new effort to sharpen the outlines of a given memory.

119. And then she had to go and start talking about him as though he lived with them, as though he'd been on her mind since the day she and my father first moved in. It was only mid-morning, she would perhaps never see him again, yet she felt he'd been there for a long time, as though she and my father had inadvertently adopted him without realizing it, and even though she had yet to hear the sound of his voice, he didn't feel strange to her; for some reason, she was sure he would turn up again and eventually talk, his words would throw a new light on their time in the villa. But then again, she was thinking, he would probably never speak to her directly, and she was going to have to live with the fact that she wouldn't understand everything he'd nevertheless be saying to her.

120. She was thinking it would be best to not tell my father. She was afraid the little being would flee, unable to take the shock of the encounter, should my father confront him, but above all she was trying to convince herself that she was completely alone with him, that no one else was aware of his existence, that no one else could care for him, get through to him, as she was sure she soon would, one way or another. She couldn't predict my father's reaction and, not being certain of him, she wasn't about to do anything hasty.

121. She saw him again, the child, the next morning, standing in the frame of the door leading to the ballroom. He was radiant. He was wearing the clothes she'd given him the day before, taking her completely by surprise. Had she already forgotten about him, had a good night's sleep been enough to erase the time they'd spent together the day before? The child was bigger than she'd thought when he was sitting on the bed. The pants and sweater were too small for him, she would have to find clothes that fit him, this time in matching colors, she thought, and he'll look even more normal, and she won't think he broke into the villa anymore, and she won't dream of contacting any asylums. All the same, it's not like he looked ridiculous. He was staring at her, or let's say it looked like he was staring at her, but it probably wasn't the case. She started thinking about the unreachable boy he'd probably always been, a little out of place in this world, the kind of child you can't send to school, and whose parents don't know what to do with anymore, or even know how to love him, mother and father at their wit's end, unsure if they should hate him or hate themselves, and maybe some brothers and sisters too, a big family, or rather a tribe with strange customs, customs that seem almost repugnant to the outside observer, a tribe living in a camper van, with grimy and taciturn children who have never once uttered the words mommy and daddy, and who seem like adults next to children their own age.

122. The idea of the tape recorder had come to her while she was looking for more clothes for him. She said to him: Follow me, in a firm voice that she hoped would be reassuring. She'd quickly gotten used to constructing her sentences carefully, so as to express herself as simply as possible, as though speaking to a foreign child learning her language. She'd realized that the possibilities were endless for expressing the most insignificant banalities, and she was always searching for the plainest way to say something. At the same time, she was forcing herself to pronounce each word—this had seemed to alter her voice, its tone, and even its texture. She'd shown him the tape recorder, explaining to him how the machine works by pushing each button several times in a row and repeating the same explanation. She'd shown him the little red light, explaining to him that whenever it was lit, the machine was recording what they were saying. And she'd given a little demonstration, which he'd followed attentively. He was apparently able to understand everything, now that she wasn't trying to get close to him.

123.

As a general rule, she was aware that people felt uncomfortable as soon as they knew their words were being recorded. Everything recorded might one day or another be held against you. But for him, she thought, it was quite the opposite. She wasn't going to keep the tapes and use them for some malign purpose. She'd only thought it would be infinitely less difficult for him to speak into a tape recorder than to a person. Was that her only motive? In any case, she was determined to communicate with him, she was ready to try anything, as long as it might help her discover what the child was looking for there.

124. Did he have a name? Was it possible to grow up without having a name? Each morning, she'd told him her own name, and she would explain that they'd been living there, she and her husband, for the past few months. They'd bought the villa, but for the time being they were having trouble living in it normally, they were going to have work done on it, after they'd thought a bit about what they could do with it. This was liable to take months, she wasn't sure how much longer it would be before they were out of the woods. It was taking longer than they'd anticipated at first. And all that was based on the assumption, for one, that they even knew what their dream house was supposed to look like. Her husband, she'd explained, pointing to the ceiling, was even now thinking about the renovations they could make; he was likely designing the layout of the interior of the refurbished villa as they spoke. It wasn't possible to see him just now (and she again made her fleeting gesture toward the ceiling), she hadn't seen much of him lately—she was telling herself it was a good sign. She was thinking it wouldn't be long now before the renovations started.

125. The sound of the cassette tape running offered another form of silence. The child still wasn't saying anything, but she was convinced he would start speaking at any moment. And given that she didn't mind the machine recording her own monologues, she was still speaking to him simply, with a kind of sincerity. He listened to her attentively for hours. It was possible that he was elsewhere, in reality she had no way of knowing if he understood her. She was never sure if she was expressing herself as simply as she would have liked.

126. Still this tormented face, slightly sad, at once frightened and frightening, as though given to expressing the entire continuum of anxiety. He looks a little like you, my mother will write.

127. They had a child too, my mother had explained, a boy who had become a man, and who was living far away, and whom they hadn't seen in years. For weeks she'd wondered what it meant "to have a child." To look at him, touch him, soothe him, whisper sweet words to him? Didn't she need him to be there next to her, in the same room, in order to "have" him? Wasn't a mother supposed to be forever making sure she still had her child, turning that contingent little being, as weak as he was, into an unwavering conviction? And ever since he'd left home, she was still without a reply. She was only too aware of his fragility, she used to think he could die at any moment. He'd needed to be alone and so, in order to guard his loneliness, he'd decided to live far away, without letting us know how he was doing. She'd told the child the clothes she'd given him were her son's. She'd kept her son's clothes, without knowing what she would do with them, and now, thanks to him, she could tell herself she'd been right to pack away his clothes. These clothes were still his, in a certain sense, but she was sure he wouldn't have minded lending his clothes to the child. He'd always been so generous, he used to throw around the pittance he would make working odd jobs— one day he would perhaps write a book, she explained. As she was folding and putting away her son's clothes in boxes, she'd felt depressed, for she was convinced she was performing a final and absurd act. She'd told herself that these clothes would never do anyone any good, and that it would've been better to give them away. She'd closed the boxes, wrapping them in adhesive tape; she'd figured she would never again need to open them to inspect their contents. She'd thought that inevitably someone would later (after she was dead) appropriate or destroy all these clothes to which not a single memory would then be attached. All of that, she'd thought, would take place in an uncertain future, so far away she was unable to really give it any thought. They'd managed not to get along with their son, she'd continued. They'd managed to not understand him. But it was probably too late to make up for any of that now.

128. Each morning, she would talk to him in the small, sun-filled room, recording their conversations. He wasn't really saying anything, but it didn't feel as though she was the only one talking, like she was talking to herself. On the contrary, she was content to prattle on, stopping at certain moments, and during these moments it was as though he was replying. Particles of dust were whirling like galaxies in front of the window. The room wasn't heated, but it was a sunny enough place to sit comfortably for an hour or two in the morning. The tape recorder would be placed on a small coffee table, plain as day. Next to the tape recorder, a carton of orange juice, their two glasses. She'd chosen a different room from the one where she'd found him. That room on the third floor—she'd felt they couldn't stand each other in it, and she wasn't sure if he'd ever gone back there, in fact, after the day she'd found him (and she wasn't exactly eager to find out either).

129.
One morning when she was too tired to improvise a conversation, she'd gotten out a photo album. She grabbed the album at random, without really knowing what she could do with it; that is, she could tell him about it, but was the child capable of focusing on images, was his brain able to make a connection between the information contained in the photo and the world to which these people, these landscapes, pointed? Every photo is a window, but that doesn't mean you always see something through it, sometimes you see nothing but vacant forms, without meaning. A photo can also be a boarded-up window. Since she'd turned the pages of this album so many times (a long time ago, now, it's true), these images were no more than allusions to a far-distant world, for her, neither present nor even past, but rather suspended between two abysses, like two fragments of time impossible to join together. She no longer believed these images were reproducing anything, and as she was looking at them, she wasn't sure anymore to which present she now belonged. But he'd started to fidget as soon as he saw the album. He was waiting for her on the threshold, like every morning, at first as quiet as a mouse, then suddenly on the alert, dimly concerned about something that he didn't quite understand. She couldn't see what was drawing his attention. They sat down, as was their habit, in the little luminous room. She poured the orange juice into glasses, in silence, careful to respect the ritual. He was waiting patiently, but she could tell he was trying to hide his extreme excitement; she was receiving the signs of his struggle as through a filter, or veil. She acknowledged the wait, its momentum, as if one's existence were sliding toward the coming moment. She put the album down on the small table and said to him: Look, turn the pages if you like. He leaned forward, rested the album on his knees, and as he began to turn the pages, carefully lifting the

sheets of parchment paper, he was almost solemn, and he seemed to be really looking at the pictures, without however lingering on any one in particular. Deckle-edged photos that were supposed to represent a foreign world in his eyes. And then he'd started talking, without her having to prod him with questions. He would close his eyes, a finger placed on a photo. She recognized the sound of his voice immediately. It wasn't exactly an imitation, but she could make out elements in his voice, his elocution, his tone, without understanding the words or grasping the meaning from the units of sound, as they flowed inside an incomprehensible monologue. She recognized this crystalline voice, at once sharp and annoying, and yet she'd never heard it before. She thought of this voice as being already dead, an unknown force having pulled it from oblivion so it could tell her certain things. All the same, she had to be thinking that her senses were perhaps playing tricks on her. She said: Pardon me? Knowing full well he wasn't listening to her. He was actually too unsettled to listen to her. He continued to speak, without appearing to care if she understood him, in his strange language. Her comprehension was not required for him to continue.

130. And what if she were to press the stop button on the tape recorder, would he break off in mid-sentence? And she was thinking about my father, who was still upstairs; he was oblivious to what was going on down here, unaware that she was now hearing his voice as it must have sounded when he was a child, unaware that she was looking for family resemblances in this face that had taken on his voice. And so she couldn't help but stare at the child, to make sure she wasn't dreaming.

131. He was sitting across from her. He hadn't moved, but he still seemed farther away than before. The photo he was looking at had been taken on the docks of the Port of Dieppe. My father had often remarked upon it the first year they were married, after she'd gotten together all the pictures to make their first photo album. She'd gathered together old black and white photographs that she'd found in various envelopes, in metal boxes. The photo was of a man in his forties. He was staring into the lens, standing on the dock. He was thin, puzzled. Behind him, the ship's hull forms an unbroken backdrop, with the letters Z É L A N, painted in white on the dark hull just above his head. If you look closely, you can make out dents in the hull, freshly repainted. She knows the story of the photograph. She could string together the two or three sentences that would reappear each time my father mentioned it. She could form a little frame out of these sentences, placing this frame around the photo as a final commentary on the scene represented in the picture. And so a motionless man poses, not for eternity, but just for the length of the voyage, slated to last several months. And since these several months also mean many miles, it appears that her father's face is already showing his coming exhaustion and uncertainty, the harshness of the work, the worry. But that's an entirely different matter. Unhinged, rambling words, and yet she understands. She understands neither the words nor the sentences they compose, she isn't even sure the words strung together form sentences at all, but she appreciates the architecture of the whole. A story that was slowly taking shape, that was appearing like a photo in a chemical solution, right up to the point where the border and shapes become sharp. She is now in the photo's world, in the cramped cabin of a ship. She is in front of a body that is hanging from a rope, she doesn't know at what point in the voyage they are; apparently the boat hasn't left the dock yet and she realizes that this man has been dead for several minutes, and she wonders why she's the one who has found him. Strangely, everything is quiet—shouldn't she be hearing the sound of the waves? She tries to think back. At the time she couldn't have been more than fourteen, and she'd never been below on a boat before. And when she would think about it, she would tell herself that she still didn't know who this man was. A movement to get herself out of this bad dream: She glanced at the window and, just then, a bird landed on the sill, pecking about. She remembered that there were bird feeders hanging in some of the windows, and that lately she was in the habit of filling them with seeds. Then the voice suddenly changed. It was no longer the annoying voice of a hysterical child, it was his voice from yesterday or the day before, his stubborn voice. He was no longer in the room, he was on the threshold of the bedroom, she couldn't see him anymore. Did you find the car keys? That is what he was saying. She made sure the tape recorder was still recording. The little red light was lit. She'd heard this sentence before, not so long ago. She wasn't trying to remember. It wasn't an act of memory—or so she told herself—no, it was more like everything was happening in the present, at this very moment, sitting across from the tape recorder, in that part of the present tense sectioned off by the cassette tape, just for them. And out of the corner of her eye, she saw something fly up from behind the glass, a brown bird with horizontal stripes, a sparrow, perhaps the bird from a moment ago, but one couldn't be sure. Next she is alone in front of the picture.

132.

She's back at the shopping center buying blank cassettes, she fills two large bags with supplies— she tends to like soft foods—raisins, packets of chewy cookies, orange juice; next she decides to buy a pair of sneakers and socks in a sporting goods store located in the center, she makes these purchases without thinking, she has to hurry, it's almost closing time. She exchanges a few pleasantries with the young cashier who is pregnant, and on the way home she's afraid she might get lost. The headlights don't give out enough light to read the markings on the signs. She should turn around and ask someone in a store at the shopping center, she says to herself, but she realizes that she forgot to get gas, and that she might run out if she goes all the way back. What she ought to do is tell herself that the villa doesn't exist, that it suddenly disappeared in the dark, swallowed by the nightmare night; there aren't any bedrooms, or corridors, the child she found never existed except in her imagination, and my father isn't waiting for her either, my father left her years ago, he has become a perfect stranger who lives with another woman and has children with his new wife, it's impossible for her to reach him, he doesn't answer the phone anymore and avoids her in the street.

133.

He doesn't send her to get his photos developed anymore, he's making himself more and more scarce. He doesn't say anything anymore. She hears his annoyed footsteps above her head.

Sébastien Brebel was born in 1971 in Argenteuil, France. He lives in Nantes where he teaches philosophy, and is the author of four novels, of which this is his first to appear in English.

Andrew Wilson is a graduate of the Master of Philosophy Program in Literary Translation at Trinity College Dublin, Ireland. He lives in Berkeley, California.

MICHAL AJVAZ, *The Golden Age.*
   The Other City.
PIERRE ALBERT-BIROT, *Grabinoulor.*
YUZ ALESHKOVSKY, *Kangaroo.*
FELIPE ALFAU, *Chromos.*
   Locos.
IVAN ÂNGELO, *The Celebration.*
   The Tower of Glass.
ANTÓNIO LOBO ANTUNES, *Knowledge of Hell.*
   The Splendor of Portugal.
ALAIN ARIAS-MISSON, *Theatre of Incest.*
JOHN ASHBERY AND JAMES SCHUYLER,
   A Nest of Ninnies.
ROBERT ASHLEY, *Perfect Lives.*
GABRIELA AVIGUR-ROTEM, *Heatwave*
   and Crazy Birds.
DJUNA BARNES, *Ladies Almanack.*
   Ryder.
JOHN BARTH, *LETTERS.*
   Sabbatical.
DONALD BARTHELME, *The King.*
   Paradise.
SVETISLAV BASARA, *Chinese Letter.*
MIQUEL BAUÇÀ, *The Siege in the Room.*
RENÉ BELLETTO, *Dying.*
MAREK BIEŃCZYK, *Transparency.*
ANDREI BITOV, *Pushkin House.*
ANDREJ BLATNIK, *You Do Understand.*
LOUIS PAUL BOON, *Chapel Road.*
   My Little War.
   Summer in Termuren.
ROGER BOYLAN, *Killoyle.*
IGNÁCIO DE LOYOLA BRANDÃO,
   Anonymous Celebrity.
   Zero.
BONNIE BREMSER, *Troia: Mexican Memoirs.*
CHRISTINE BROOKE-ROSE, *Amalgamemnon.*
BRIGID BROPHY, *In Transit.*
GERALD L. BRUNS, *Modern Poetry and*
   the Idea of Language.
GABRIELLE BURTON, *Heartbreak Hotel.*
MICHEL BUTOR, *Degrees.*
   Mobile.
G. CABRERA INFANTE, *Infante's Inferno.*
   Three Trapped Tigers.
JULIETA CAMPOS,
   The Fear of Losing Eurydice.
ANNE CARSON, *Eros the Bittersweet.*
ORLY CASTEL-BLOOM, *Dolly City.*
LOUIS-FERDINAND CÉLINE, *Castle to Castle.*
   Conversations with Professor Y.
   London Bridge.
   Normance.
   North.
   Rigadoon.
MARIE CHAIX, *The Laurels of Lake Constance.*
HUGO CHARTERIS, *The Tide Is Right.*
ERIC CHEVILLARD, *Demolishing Nisard.*
MARC CHOLODENKO, *Mordechai Schamz.*
JOSHUA COHEN, *Witz.*
EMILY HOLMES COLEMAN, *The Shutter*
   of Snow.
ROBERT COOVER, *A Night at the Movies.*
STANLEY CRAWFORD, *Log of the S.S. The*
   Mrs Unguentine.
   Some Instructions to My Wife.
RENÉ CREVEL, *Putting My Foot in It.*
RALPH CUSACK, *Cadenza.*
NICHOLAS DELBANCO, *The Count of Concord.*
   Sherbrookes.
NIGEL DENNIS, *Cards of Identity.*

PETER DIMOCK, *A Short Rhetoric for*
   Leaving the Family.
ARIEL DORFMAN, *Konfidenz.*
COLEMAN DOWELL,
   Island People.
   Too Much Flesh and Jabez.
ARKADII DRAGOMOSHCHENKO, *Dust.*
RIKKI DUCORNET, *The Complete*
   Butcher's Tales.
   The Fountains of Neptune.
   The Jade Cabinet.
   Phosphor in Dreamland.
WILLIAM EASTLAKE, *The Bamboo Bed.*
   Castle Keep.
   Lyric of the Circle Heart.
JEAN ECHENOZ, *Chopin's Move.*
STANLEY ELKIN, *A Bad Man.*
   Criers and Kibitzers, Kibitzers
   and Criers.
   The Dick Gibson Show.
   The Franchiser.
   The Living End.
   Mrs. Ted Bliss.
FRANÇOIS EMMANUEL, *Invitation to a*
   Voyage.
SALVADOR ESPRIU, *Ariadne in the*
   Grotesque Labyrinth.
LESLIE A. FIEDLER, *Love and Death in*
   the American Novel.
JUAN FILLOY, *Op Oloop.*
ANDY FITCH, *Pop Poetics.*
GUSTAVE FLAUBERT, *Bouvard and Pécuchet.*
KASS FLEISHER, *Talking out of School.*
FORD MADOX FORD,
   The March of Literature.
JON FOSSE, *Aliss at the Fire.*
   Melancholy.
MAX FRISCH, *I'm Not Stiller.*
   Man in the Holocene.
CARLOS FUENTES, *Christopher Unborn.*
   Distant Relations.
   Terra Nostra.
   Where the Air Is Clear.
TAKEHIKO FUKUNAGA, *Flowers of Grass.*
WILLIAM GADDIS, *J R.*
   The Recognitions.
JANICE GALLOWAY, *Foreign Parts.*
   The Trick Is to Keep Breathing.
WILLIAM H. GASS, *Cartesian Sonata*
   and Other Novellas.
   Finding a Form.
   A Temple of Texts.
   The Tunnel.
   Willie Masters' Lonesome Wife.
GÉRARD GAVARRY, *Hoppla! 1 2 3.*
ETIENNE GILSON,
   The Arts of the Beautiful.
   Forms and Substances in the Arts.
C. S. GISCOMBE, *Giscome Road.*
   Here.
DOUGLAS GLOVER, *Bad News of the Heart.*
WITOLD GOMBROWICZ,
   A Kind of Testament.
PAULO EMÍLIO SALES GOMES, *P's Three*
   Women.
GEORGI GOSPODINOV, *Natural Novel.*
JUAN GOYTISOLO, *Count Julian.*
   Juan the Landless.
   Makbara.
   Marks of Identity.

SELECTED DALKEY ARCHIVE TITLES

SELECTED DALKEY ARCHIVE TITLES

DUMITRU TSEPENEAG, *Hotel Europa*.
  The Necessary Marriage.
  Pigeon Post.
  Vain Art of the Fugue.
ESTHER TUSQUETS, *Stranded*.
DUBRAVKA UGRESIC, *Lend Me Your Character*.
  Thank You for Not Reading.
TOR ULVEN, *Replacement*.
MATI UNT, *Brecht at Night*.
  Diary of a Blood Donor.
  Things in the Night.
ÁLVARO URIBE AND OLIVIA SEARS, EDS.,
  Best of Contemporary Mexican Fiction.
ELOY URROZ, *Friction*.
  The Obstacles.
LUISA VALENZUELA, *Dark Desires and
  the Others*.
  He Who Searches.
PAUL VERHAEGHEN, *Omega Minor*.
AGLAJA VETERANYI, *Why the Child Is
  Cooking in the Polenta*.
BORIS VIAN, *Heartsnatcher*.
LLORENÇ VILLALONGA, *The Dolls' Room*.
TOOMAS VINT, *An Unending Landscape*.
ORNELA VORPSI, *The Country Where No
  One Ever Dies*.
AUSTRYN WAINHOUSE, *Hedyphagetica*.
CURTIS WHITE, *America's Magic Mountain*.
  The Idea of Home.
  Memories of My Father Watching TV.
  Requiem.

DIANE WILLIAMS, *Excitability:
  Selected Stories*.
  Romancer Erector.
DOUGLAS WOOLF, *Wall to Wall*.
  Ya! & John-Juan.
JAY WRIGHT, *Polynomials and Pollen*.
  *The Presentable Art of Reading
  Absence*.
PHILIP WYLIE, *Generation of Vipers*.
MARGUERITE YOUNG, *Angel in the Forest*.
  Miss MacIntosh, My Darling.
REYOUNG, *Unbabbling*.
VLADO ŽABOT, *The Succubus*.
ZORAN ŽIVKOVIĆ, *Hidden Camera*.
LOUIS ZUKOFSKY, *Collected Fiction*.
VITOMIL ZUPAN, *Minuet for Guitar*.
SCOTT ZWIREN, *God Head*.